MAFIA BEAST
A DARK MAFIA ROMANCE

SHANNA HANDEL

WELCOME

Mafia Beast: A Dark Mafia Romance

Shanna Handel

I'll teach her what happens to naughty girls.

She never should have spied on me.

My punishments left her burning with shame…

Needing more.

Pain from her past made her run from me.

Now I've found out she's hidden a secret.

One she never should have tried to keep from me.

I won't allow it.

She will be mine.

I'll use force to take what belongs to me.

I'm known for my massive size. I can give her what she needs.

I'll make her my wife.

I will make her love me.

Copyright © 2022 Shanna Handel

All rights reserved.

Credits to my wonderful team:

Artwork by Pop Kitty Design

Photography by

WANDER AGUIAR PHOTOGRAPHY LLC

Editing by Jane Beyer

Proofread by Julie Barney

Beta Reader & ARC Director Jess Bracewell

CHAPTER ONE

Charlie

I reach out to grab another flute of champagne from a passing tray. I really shouldn't. I've already had one. After skipping lunch to make sure this event went off without so much as a petal out of place, the alcohol is going straight to my head. I raise the glass toward my mouth, the blush pink polish on my nails sparkling under the ballroom lights.

The angel on my left shoulder debates with the little hot pink she-devil on my right.

Who's here to stop you? the little she-devil whispers, tipping the glass against my lips with her golden pitchfork. *You've lost every man that you've ever loved. Cursed them all with a death sentence.*

Their only crime?

Loving me.

I'm being dramatic. Little she-devil wins. I tilt the glass, sending the cold bubbly liquid down my throat. Half a flute in one swallow.

A gorgeous couple walks by, the husband's hand casually lowering from his wife's waist to cup her curvy ass in her silky black gown. She sighs, leaning into her man with blissful contentment. So. *Sexy.* My core aches with jealousy. I tip my unquenched desires back with the glass, polishing off the champagne.

Food and drink are the only swallowing I've been doing these past seven years. I'm practically a born-again virgin. Is it possible for cobwebs to grow there? I start to giggle.

Now I really am tipsy. Time for making bad decisions. I glance around the room at the elegant couples celebrating our annual Winter Ball. Like most of our family functions, almost every single man is attached. There's a cluster of ridiculously good-looking younger brothers at the bar, their heads leaning toward one another as they joke over their shots of expensive whiskey. Gorgeous but not my type. There is no one here for me.

Who am I trying to kid anyway? I'm a good girl. Even two glasses of champagne can't change that major character flaw that resides deep within the core of my being: I almost always do the right thing. The most my little she-devil ever convinces me of is to overindulge in chocolate or champagne, hence the battle I got into with the zipper of my dress earlier this evening.

I won, but I am moving very gingerly tonight.

There's a flower wall of chocolates across the room. The brainchild of me, a chocolate addict. Poking out from the real, green leaves and lush heads of multicolored roses are little shelves, each holding a different treat from New York's current hottest chocolatier, *Lush*.

If I can't make mistakes with a man, I can at least inhale too many sweets. That should satisfy this naughty streak that seems to be running through me as of late.

My Christian Louboutin Kate pumps click across the polished wood floor as I make my way over to my magnificent creation. They're turquoise with sparkles to go with the aqua dress I've chosen for tonight. I went with a mermaid-feel, leaving my floral prints behind. The aquamarine silk slides against my skin as I move, as smooth and cool as a current of river water.

Just eyeing the little rosettes of candies makes my mouth water. I know there's a rich, creamy caramel hidden inside the shiny chocolate shell. I reach for one but before I can wrap my greedy fingers around it, Emilia's whispering in my ear.

Her blonde curls bounce, the signature scent of Chanel Coco Mademoiselle swirling around me as her words tickle my skin. "Don't look now, but *he's* here." Just the way she pronounces "he's" in that honeyed tone makes my knees go weak.

"Him?" I stare at her. Her eyes sparkle as she nods. "I didn't even know he was in New York. He wasn't supposed to come." My gaze darts around the room, looking for his massive frame. I can't find him.

Emilia grabs my hand, tugging me behind the leafy wall. My eyes go to the wiring that snakes through the back of the frame.

"How did they do this?" I take a quick second to try to figure out the magic of their craft. I file away the craftsmanship for the next party, determined to create my own. "Isn't it incredible?"

"Yeah. It's great." She peeks out from behind the wall, looking for *him*.

Am I stalling or really curious about the display's construction? "Almost an illusion, isn't it?" I reach out, tugging at a wire, not quite ready to discuss *him*. Subject change. I gesture at the wall with my full arm, like a game show attendant, flashing Emilia a bright grin. "Amazing how they took my simple vision and made it real."

"Huh?" Emilia's light brow knits as she stares at me. "What are you talking about?"

"The dessert wall," I say. "It's just amazing how they made the chocolates look as if they're floating among the flowers."

Her dark lashes flutter toward the wall. "Oh, yes. It's very nice. But did you hear what I said?" She grabs my arm, her fingers digging lightly into my skin in her attempt to bring me back to the moment. "*He's* here."

There's that tone again, making the little hairs on the back of my neck stand on end. A tickle rises in the back of my throat. My fingers flutter at my clavicle, heat rushing under my skin. I try to avoid revealing my curiosity in the tone of my voice. "I haven't seen him. Haven't thought about him... really."

Emilia rolls her eyes. "Haven't you? Anyway... I heard that he was asking about you after the fundraiser at the Hamlet—"

"There you both are! I've been looking everywhere for you." Kylie pops behind the wall, tossing her long dark hair over a bare shoulder, the straps of her sparkly red gown no more than beaded threads. She grabs my hand in hers, tugging me toward her. "Did you hear? *He's* here. I thought for sure he'd have come over to you by now, the way he was asking about you back in Connecticut—"

"Well, he hasn't. And to be honest, I'm glad." The heat creeps upward, burning my cheeks and tingling at my hairline. "I really am not looking to get involved with anyone."

"You don't have to get involved, per se." Emilia gives a naughty little wink. "Just have a little taste test."

"A taste?" I flash her a grin. "Really?"

Kylie chimes in. "Besides, we're all so curious about... you know..." Blinking rapidly, Kylie makes a circular gesture below her waist. "You know."

"What?" I ask, not giving her the satisfaction of participating in such a ridiculous discussion.

"You know what we're talking about." Emilia elbows my ribs, waggling her brow. "His... size."

Standing six foot five with shoulders that fill a doorway, I know it's not the man's striking physique they're talking about. Whispers of his... penis... have been floating through the Beauties ever since he joined the family.

"And what does his size have to do with me?" Please don't let me be blushing as hard as I think I am.

"Come on!" Emilia croons. "You're single. He's single. We can't find out ourselves. He's obviously interested. Besides, we Beauties kind of have bets going on. You could settle them for us."

Have they seriously been discussing his size? I can't believe this. "Bets? Really?"

Kylie gives a serious nod. "Yes, there's actually been quite a bit of arguing lately. Some feel that it isn't humanly possible to be that big—"

"Mainly Hannah the scientist," Emilia adds.

"Right. It's like, don't always be so logical, Hannah. Sometimes you just gotta believe." Kylie rolls her eyes.

Emilia's voice drops to a hushed whisper. "Others have said they've heard it's true."

The heat is cranking up in this room. I pull a stray leaf off the back of the wall, fanning myself with it. "Well. Oh my. Dear me."

If it's anything close to the size of the rest of him...

They start to argue amongst themselves, talking about a friend of a Beauty who apparently has had the pleasure. The racy image they plant in my mind turns the prickly heat on my skin to an inferno.

I pull away from them. "Oh my gosh. I can't believe this is even a conversation we are having. Leave me out of it, please. I am so not interested."

I move toward the exit. I need air.

Emilia and Kylie's hushed whispers and silly giggles trail behind me as I make my way toward the open door of the terrace. It's unseasonably warm tonight and a gentle breeze instantly cools my skin, my hair swirling around my shoulders. It's a moonless evening. The sky would be an inky black but in the city that never sleeps, I'm surrounded by the soft orange and white glow from the lit buildings.

It's noisier here than I remember, sirens and car horns blaring into the night.

I've grown used to the quiet sounds of Liam's bachelor pad, an Italian lakeside estate where I've been living, my peaceful escape from the dozens of happily married couples in the Village. I did all his decorating for him.

Since his marriage to Emilia, he no longer needs my help. They begged me to stay but nothing rubs salt into the wound of my loneliness like living with two hot-to-trot newlyweds who can't keep their hands off one another.

It's good to be back in the Village. Right?

Our family is a secret mafia, the Robin Hood of bad guys, stealing from the rich and giving to the poor. Men get in through a grueling initiation process. Women, only by marriage. And the unlucky few of us who become widows, well, we still have a place in the family. Being a Bachman is for life.

Our hub, our base of operations, is this Village. Entirely surrounded by a gray stone wall, it's the size of a full city block. Behind the backs of the windowless buildings that surround the wall are dozens of double-entry black gates, a security pad used to open them.

The businesses and shops that form the square are all owned by the family. Each with their own secret closet in the back of an office, storeroom, or cloak closet, concealing blocked exits accessible only to Bachmans.

The housing is gorgeous, all row homes, three stories each. Seven homes to a street, and seven streets. Each structure is identical, except each individual makes their place their own with paint color, gardening, and landscaping. Large windows are on both the western and eastern sides of the homes, and also open to the back gardens and the streets. The perfectly manicured streets are tree-lined, with one main park in the center.

We have a rooftop bar, a schoolroom, cafes, and most recently added, this events center.

As I gaze over the balcony, I find my fingers tightening around the railing of the terrace, feeling like I'm lost, like I'm floating since I've been back. I know I need to join the others...

Speaking of...The first notes of "Rock the Boat" beat through the night. Peals of laughter fill the air. I turn back toward the ballroom, watching as a rainbow of Beauties make their way to the dance floor.

Newlywed Shannon taught everyone this funny dance they do back in her hometown in Ireland whenever this song comes on. She made us do it at her wedding reception and everyone loved it. Soon, the women are sitting on the floor in lines—thousands of dollars of designer-labeled gowns be damned—rocking forward and back in one another's arms like they're rowing a boat as they perform the dance.

I should join them…

An angry shout from the street grabs my attention. My gaze leaves the cheery ballroom. From where I stand on the terrace, I can see just over the black gate between the brownstone buildings, out onto the street. The cooling effects of the breeze instantly dissipate as a massive, familiar shape steps out of the shadows.

It's *him*.

The Beast.

So he is here…

Just the sight of him makes my heart beat faster, heat spreading from my face down through my belly, warming between my thighs. Shame fills me as I shift my weight from foot to foot.

Get yourself together, Charlie.

It was one dance.

One special moment at Kylie's wedding reception that's forever encapsulated in my memory.

If I close my eyes, I can still feel the way his huge hand splayed out across my lower back, his other holding mine in such a possessive way I had to lower my gaze. We barely spoke, but there wasn't a hint of awkwardness between us. Just a burning sexual tension, from my side at least. I can only flatter myself to assume he felt it too.

Beauty dancing with her Beast.

Actually, I know he felt it too because he called me after that event. Every day. And asked me out. Every day. I turned him down. Every day. At the time, this Beauty, though intrigued by the Beast, wasn't ready for the intensity I knew he would bring.

And, yes, the Beast has a name. Nikolaos Bachman, fresh from Greece. The brothers' latest recruit. He currently oversees security in our town, the Hamlet, in Connecticut.

He stands with his massive biceps crossed over the wide plane of his chest. Dressed in a short-sleeved, deep-green button-down tucked into black pants, a thick black belt around his waist and heavy black boots on his feet, his clothes evoke an air worthy of his military background. He runs his thick fingers over his full beard as he eyes the street.

On tiptoe, I stretch my neck, straining to see over the gate. What's he looking at? With extensive military training as an Air Martial in Greece's military, he sees something that's invisible to me.

What in the world is going on down there? We're told to stay out of the brothers' business. If we see something that gives off even a hint of violence or danger, we are to immediately head in the opposite direction.

But the compass in my belly is pulling me toward the action, toward the street. That naughty streak that keeps rearing its little kitten head pops up, the little pink she-devil whispering to me, *Don't you want to go see what's happening?*

Curiosity killed the cat, I snap back.

Your pussy's been neglected for so long your cat is already dead, the little she-devil shoots back in return.

Fine. I'll go.

My belly flip-flops as I make my way down to the street. There's one emotion I can't deny — I find the man incredibly intriguing.

CHAPTER TWO

Beast
What's this?

Charlie Bachman, the button-nosed Beauty whose wide hazel eyes hold a world of innocence waiting to be corrupted. What's she doing here, peeking out from behind the unlatched gate? She thinks she's hidden from my view but she's not aware of the bubble mirror hanging above her head. One glance and I can see her in her entirety, hiding behind the gate.

Throwing a wrench in my plans. Threatening to expose my cover. Every Bachman other than the top three in the chain of command believes I'm a security guard for the Hamlet. I'm not. For the sake of everyone involved, it's better that everyone continues to believe that.

I'm not going to let a nosy little girl mess this up.

Not that there's anything girlish about her tonight. She's all woman, a beacon of femininity and sex appeal. The way her floor-length silk dress hugs her curves makes my mouth water. The aquamarine color of the material reminds me of the deep teal colors of the Aegean Sea back home in Greece. The shade conjures up an image of her lying on my white sand beaches, my fingers slowly peeling the silk back, exposing her lovely breasts...

"Are we going to do this or what?" The punk's nasal voice brings me back to my present situation. Everything about him, from his disheveled hair to his imitation leather jacket, screams jackass. He taps his bootheel against the pavement of the sidewalk with impatience. "I haven't got all night."

"You might not have any of the night left if you don't calm down." I'm careful to keep my gaze away from where Charlie hides, not wanting him to know we have a visitor.

"Ha." He takes a step toward me. "Is that a challenge?"

Mistake. He's young and overconfident. Two things that can get a person killed around here. And he's getting agitated. Agitation is bad. It makes people do impulsive things. Our deal is very temperamental, dancing on a wire. It doesn't need the added weight of impulsivity. When I first met this kid, my gut told me to pass on him. But it's hard to find the connections we need in the world we're trying to enter.

I'll have to take my chances. But I can't deal with this prick with Charlie here. What I really want to do is deal with Charlie.

I hate the thought of missing a shipment. The thought of delaying tears at my gut. For whatever reason, since the first time I laid eyes on Charlie Bachman, she's moved to the forefront of my thoughts. Tonight, she comes first.

She'll have to be taught a lesson. She, like every other Beauty here tonight, knows not to get involved in back-alley disputes. Now I'm feeling agitated, my hand itching to discipline her generous curves.

I glance from his patchy-bearded face back to her corner. I need to be rid of him. But if he gets pissed off and tries to act tough, I'll have to hurt him. I don't want to do that in front of Charlie.

Dilemmas.

His eyes flash as he slips his hand into his pocket, no doubt to retrieve a weapon to threaten me with. I need to react, but now, with the little mermaid having come to spy on me, everything I've built is at risk.

I step toward him, locking a hand around one of his shoulders and grabbing his wrist before he can pull his hand from his pocket. Keeping my mouth close to his ear and my voice low, I tell him exactly what will happen to him if he doesn't turn around and walk away. Right now.

"What about our deal?" he growls back.

"It's off for now. I'll be in touch. Take care of the goods until I can get them, or I swear, this night will be your last." I dig my fingers into his shoulder before giving him a shove toward the street. "Go. Now."

His youthful overconfidence dances in his irises. He's deciding whether he's going to try to do something stupid to keep his ego from getting bruised, or instead save his body from the bruises that will come with his obstinance.

I round my shoulders and give him a glare to help him make up his mind.

"Fine." He shoots me a look of disgust before turning on his heel. "I'll be in touch."

Now, to deal with my naughty Beauty.

There's a skittering sound from behind the gate — red-soled sparkly stilettos hitting pavement in an attempt to get back to the party before me. Does she really think she's gotten away with her little adventure?

How to play this...

Call her name? Creep up on her and surprise her? See the terror on her face when she realizes she's been caught. Her full lips falling open in shock. Plan B makes my cock throb.

Surprise it is.

Without a sound I move toward the partially opened gate. She's pressing her thumb against the security panel, trying to get the second gate to open, the one that would let her escape to the safety of the Village. I installed a manual lock on it when I came out here to meet the punk so family members could get out, but no one could get in until I reset it.

I watch with amusement as she frantically pushes her thumb on the pad over and over. Wait for it... three... two... one... Her lovely face turns over her shoulder to find *me*.

And there it is. The shamefully sexy look of being caught. A flush instantly rises in her cheeks, her beautiful eyes going wide as saucers. Her full lips, stained a deep red for the occasion, fall open, and I go hard as a rock knowing in just a moment, I'll be using them as part of her punishment.

"Naughty girl." My deep voice rumbles through the small enclosure. I pull the gate to the street closed behind me. The whir of the mechanics purrs through the night as it locks. Now it's just me and her locked in between the two gates, thick stone walls on either side of us. "Putting your nose where it doesn't belong, and now you're trapped."

She flips around, pressing her back against the tall black gate. Her palms curl around the iron bars of the gate behind her. She shakes her head, stammering her excuses while inching her way over to the wall. "I was on the balcony overlooking the street. I just... I heard voices and..."

"And you thought you'd come down here and explore?"

Her pearly white teeth sink into her bottom lip, and she nods.

Brave of her to come out and admit it. Not try to make up some elaborate excuse about how she dropped an earring. "Honesty. I like it. But please, use your words."

"I was... curious, sir."

Sir. My cock pulses at the word. I love a good girl who knows how to correctly address the man she's in trouble with.

"And where did curiosity get the cat, little girl?"

Fear flashes through her gaze and she gives a hard swallow, her pink fingernails shining as she twists her hands together. "Killed... sir?"

I have to chuckle at her obvious terror. "Good thing you're not a cat, isn't it? But you are a naughty little minx. Do you know what curiosity gets the naughty little girl?"

Her teeth sink back into those perfect lips as she shakes her head.

"Punishments."

Her dark lashes flutter as she blinks back my threat. "P—punishments? Plural?"

My gaze drags across those red lips. "Yes. Plural."

She tries to press herself further against the wall as if it will melt like the chocolate she loves so much, enveloping her and saving her from me. No such luck. The wall is stone and as hard as my cock is about to be. She's all mine and as trapped as she can be. My own little taste of dessert. I don't know why I get so much satisfaction from punishing a beautiful, naughty woman, but I do.

As I saunter toward her she gives a little jump of fright with each step of my boots. My cock seems to jerk in time with her movements. Her eyes go glassy, shining with the fear of what's about to happen, her breaths quickening at the uncertainty of what's to become of her. My blood heats, pumping through my veins at an accelerated rate. I grab her wrist with one hand, her waist with the other.

"Ooof!" She gives a little shriek as I turn her to face the wall. Her skin is warm under mine, reminding me of that dance we had at the Hamlet, her body pressed against me. I want that feeling again now. I crowd her, pressing my chest against her back, my aching erection into the cleft of her ass.

God, she feels so good wrapped in the protective cocoon of my body, though I'm the one she needs protection from. I think of her cute little button nose poking into my business, putting herself in danger, and I can't help but to drag my hand up her thigh, grabbing her ass, hard.

She pops up on tiptoe, squealing as my fingers dig into the soft curves of her flesh.

"Surely you knew I would find you here. And that I would punish you." My fingertips drag the silky material of her dress up, gathering it in my palm in bunches. Glancing down, I get a flash of her bare skin, glowing under the streetlight.

Her ass is every bit as gorgeous as I knew it would be, the material of her dress so thin it leaves little to the imagination. I suck in a hiss of a breath... No panties. God damn. I run my hand over her curves.

"Do you always make a habit of not wearing panties?"

"The dress didn't allow for them," she shoots back.

"Makes my job easier." And my cock even harder.

Pulling back, I give her ass a most satisfying slap with my open palm. With a shriek, she shoots up on tiptoe again. I watch as the print of my hand blooms pink on her skin.

"And what makes you think this is your job?" Her question ends in a squeal. "To discipline me?"

"Who else is going to do it?" That sassy tone won't last much longer. A few more good, hard spanks should do the trick. I slap her ass again, harder this time, right in the same spot as the first spank. She gives a pretty little cry, rolling her hips. "Besides, I'm the one you were spying on. So it falls under my jurisdiction." Lucky me.

I spank her again, putting a matching print on her other cheek. God, she looks good wearing my mark.

"Oooh…" she groans, shifting her weight from foot to foot. Her curls bounce as she snaps her gaze over her shoulder to meet mine. "That hurt!"

Her hazel eyes flash with accusation. I don't bother trying to hold in the chuckle that bubbles up from my chest. She's too fucking adorable.

"What did you expect?" I slap her ass again and again, till her voice is replaced with a high-pitched, sexy whine. I can't help myself. I run my opened palms over the curves of her ass, exploring the roundness, the fullness of her.

She moans, easing into my touch. "Oh… my…"

Her skin is warm and red and so fucking sexy from the spanking I just gave her. I said punishments, plural. And I've been staring at that pretty little mouth of hers all night.

I can't wait any longer.

My fingers go to my belt, the metal clacking as I unfasten its buckle. "Now get down on your knees and take me in your mouth. *All* of me."

Her perfectly manicured brow knits together in disbelief. "Who do you think you are? To treat me like this? I mean, I spied on you, and you punished me. Fine. But I barely know you other than sharing one dance, and you think I'm going to..." Her pretty lips can't say the filthy words.

I finish the thought for her. "Suck my cock. Yes."

My words make her cheeks flush as rosy as her spanked ass. "What makes you think I'm going to kneel down in this way and..." The blush deepens as she tries to think of a way around saying the words. She settles on, "What makes you think I'm going to kneel down and do what you just said?"

"Easy."

She throws those perfectly manicured hands to her hips, a sudden breeze of bravery filling her. Her brows go sky high and her tone demanding. "Enlighten me."

I take a finger, dragging it over the low neckline of her silky dress, tracing over the curve of her breast, circling her hardening nipple. She gives a gasp at my touch. "Because you don't get to come if you don't do what I say."

Her pretty lips drop open. My cock jolts. I want inside her warm, wet mouth. Now. She's kept me waiting long enough.

My hand goes to her shoulder, gently pressing her down to the ground. She looks up at me, startled, like she can't believe this is happening, but with the grace of a dancer, she folds at the knees, ruining her pretty dress as she balances on the pavement.

I won't leave her there for long. I don't want her knees in pain. I just want to know what it feels like to fuck her gorgeous mouth.

Her eyes look up at me, wide and filled with trepidation, yet trusting. I undo my pants, slowly lower the zipper—I never wear anything beneath, commando is the way I like it—and free my steadily growing cock from my trousers.

She gasps. Out loud. Actually chokes on her breath at the sight of it. Her pretty fingers go to her mouth, pink fingernails fluttering as she takes me in. She mumbles something incoherent to me with her hand covering her mouth, but it sounds a bit like, "All bets are off."

I don't know what she's on about and I don't care. My cock is throbbing, and I need to feel her lips and tongue wrapped around it. "Take it in your mouth. All of it."

At my command, her nipples harden under the thin material of her dress. The sight of her taut nipples almost makes me come. "Open," I say, guiding my cock toward her pretty pout.

Finally, I get the moment I've been craving. I slide my hard cock into her warm, wet, obedient mouth, her tongue swirling against my bare skin, her lips locking around me. It's fucking amazing. I can't hold back the groan as my eyes close.

All the tension leaves my body, seeping into the pavement as she gags on my massive cock. They call me the Beast for many reasons and the size of my dick is one of them. I cup my balls in my hand, playing with them as she struggles to take more of me into her mouth. I grab the hair at the back of her head in my hand, balling it into my fist. I guide her up and down my long, thick shaft till she's gagging.

Fuck. She feels so fucking good. She's going to make me come. But I'm not done with her yet. The moment I caught her spying, I knew

I was going to be buried deep inside her pussy before this night was over.

"Enough." I pull away from her suddenly, jerking my cock from her mouth, leaving her lurching forward, her hands going to the tops of her thighs to steady herself.

"Now put your hands against the wall," I say. "I'm going to fuck you so hard you can't walk straight."

CHAPTER
THREE

Charlie

I can't believe it's true. He's every bit as big as the rumors insinuated he was. I should know — I tried to take the entirety of that massive thing down my throat, and I'm still gagging back watery tears. And now, he wants to put that giant thing... *inside* of me?

Will it even fit?

I don't think so. But the look of determination in his steely gaze says he's going to make it fit. Incoming air hitches in the back of my throat, choking me.

Can't breathe. Can't think. My hands obediently press against the cool stone of the wall. My head goes dizzy with disbelief. I can't believe this is happening...

I'm going to get... *fucked*... in an alleyway... by the Beast.

Hot pink she-devil grins. *Yes, you are, girl, yes you are. It's about damn time someone fucked you.*

"Let's see how wet you are." His big fingers walk between the soft flesh of my inner thighs, finding my pussy.

I can't hold back the moan that rises from my core as his fingers sweep over my sex. I'm not just wet for him. I'm positively dripping.

He gives a groan of desire as he slips his slickened fingers over my clit. My back arches, my knees turning to jelly as he pushes one thick finger inside of me. He pumps it, and my hips buck.

"Want more, don't you, greedy girl?"

He adds a second finger to the first, making me gasp. The pad of his thumb sweeps over my clit, sending an electric pulse jolting through my body.

"Answer me. You want more, greedy girl? You want my cock inside of you?"

The words fall from my mouth as his fingers move inside me. "Yes, God, yes."

His cock is still hard, wet from my mouth. The head of it presses between my ass cheeks, pressing on my asshole.

"Whoa there, beastie boy!" My head flips over my shoulder. "Wrong spot."

He gives a dark, foreboding chuckle. "Not today. But one day."

White-hot heat creeps over my skin. Is he serious? No one has ever been there before...

My thoughts dissipate as his cock finds the entrance to my pussy.

"Oh God..." It feels so good already, just the very tip of his cock pressing against me.

He grabs my hips, pulling them to him, slamming his cock into my wet, waiting pussy. My nails scratch at the wall, wanting something to grip, something to grab, something to anchor me to this world.

I choke back a cry, his cock gagging me as he enters me from the back almost as it did when it was in my mouth. He's so, so big. Filling me, stretching me, making my skin burn with a heat that travels all the way through my limbs.

The warmth flushes my skin, perspiration prickles at my hairline.

His hands are all over me at once, grabbing my breasts, pinching my nipples, rubbing my clit. He pulls back, thrusting inside of me again. So. Big. My back arches like a cat, my ass slamming against him. My mouth falls open, a strangled cry piercing the night.

I'm so turned on by his punishments, his words, his touch, it's not going to take much more for me to come. My heart rate accelerates, my breaths come faster. My eyelids squeeze shut, tight. The orgasm grows with each one of his hard thrusts of ownership. He possesses my body, my mind, my pleasure. The climax comes hard and fast, tearing through me, tightening every muscle in my body, holding me captive, until finally...

Sweet release.

His fingers dig into my hips so hard I know I'll find bruises tomorrow. He breathes my name like he's praying to God. "Charlie, sweet Charlie." With a staggering groan, he plants his cock deep inside of me, climaxing with a hot spew of cum.

I pant, palms sweaty against the wall, my forehead resting on my forearm, hot cum running down the inside of my thigh.

His teeth nip at my ear, his breath warm against my flesh, sending those tiny hairs at the back of my neck to stand on end. His voice is gruff, but the words are soft. "I want to see you again."

"What?" I didn't expect this. I turn over my shoulder and our eyes meet. Time takes a beat, the air goes still, and something moves inside of me as we hold our gazes locked to one another.

There's desire behind his hard gaze and it tears me apart.

I have to say no.

I can't do to him what I did to the other two.

"No." I shake my head. "I'm sorry, but it's not possible."

"We'll see." He stares at me, his gaze telling me this isn't over. He tucks himself back into his trousers, righting his belt buckle as I try to straighten my disaster of a dress. I can't believe the zipper held.

On wobbly tiptoe, I plant a soft kiss on his cheek. "Goodbye."

He grabs me, pulling me into him. His lips find mine, kissing all the chasteness from them, lighting a fire as his tongue sweeps mine. The kiss makes me dizzy and heady with endorphins. He releases me, stepping back.

"We'll see," he repeats, opening the gate for me.

I can feel his heated gaze on me as I walk away.

I do my best to walk straight but it's sore and slick between my legs.

I would love nothing more than to just walk straight home, to not see anyone. But Emilia and Kylie will be worried about me. I'll say a quick goodbye to them, then go clean up.

I keep to the walls, the shadows, not wanting anyone to see me like this. I find them standing by the champagne fountain, filling their glasses.

"Psst." I hiss to get their attention, waving my hand to them, beckoning.

They stare at me, their mouths gaping.

They've never seen me with so much as a wrinkle in my blouse. Now, I stand hiding behind a pillar with my disheveled hair. What once was sexy, smoky eye makeup I'm sure is now smudged under my eyes like raccoon rings. My red lipstick is probably circling my lips like a birthday clown.

They come rushing over.

Emilia gives a harsh whisper, taking in my altered state. "My God, Charlie, what happened to you?"

"Well, girls." I stare back, throwing my hands on my hips for effect. "Settle the bets. It's true." If their jaws could drop any further, they'd be on the floor. "Like, *way* true," I add.

And with that, I click-clack away on my heels, leaving the room before they even come to from my revelation.

I can't talk about him with them. I shouldn't even be thinking about him. I'm going home to my townhouse for a nice, long, *cold* shower.

After what he did to me... the spanking, making me kneel down on the ground and take his massive... She-devil whispers, *come on, you can say it.*

Cock... in my mouth, then taking me up against the wall like that...

Shame settles around me like a hot blanket. There was something so sexy, so powerful about being out of control, about doing what he said, about pleasing him. For a girl who won't leave the house with a chipped nail, how was it a turn-on to have my knees digging into the pavement, my dress destroyed, my lips left swollen from his use?

And the sex. My goodness, the sex. I've never come so hard in my life.

I think I saw God...

I definitely saw heaven, bright white stars flashing behind my lids as my body left this Earth.

But it will have to be the first and last time he makes me come.

This Beauty has no business getting tangled up with a Beast like him.

And in this moment, sore from his massive cock, slickness rubbing between my thighs, I realize...

We didn't use a condom.

CHAPTER
FOUR
AROUND THREE MONTHS LATER

Beast

I'm a member of the most powerful mafia in New York and, quite possibly, the world. I'm six foot five, made of solid muscle. People cross the street when they see me coming, terrified of my presence.

So why am I feeling shaky as I'm pulling up her contact info? It's a simple phone call.

She picks up on the second ring. "Hello?"

"Hey." The sound of her voice stills my nerves. I lay out on my sofa, getting comfortable. "How are you?"

"Just as well as the last time you called. Last week. And the week before that." She sounds like she's holding back a giggle. "Nothing's really changed."

I call her every week. I get rejected, every week. I just want to hear her voice, to know what she's been doing with her time. And yes...

I'd like to fuck her.

I stretch out, throwing my arm behind the back of my head. I put the phone to speaker, laying it on the cushion beside me. "Talk to me. Tell me what you've been up to."

"Oh, you know…" She gives a little sigh. "Let me think. I've been busy with all the event planning for the Village. You know how the family loooves their parties."

"I know," I say. "I particularly enjoyed the Winter Ball."

The part where you sucked me off in the alleyway, I think to myself. I reach down, stroking my cock through my jeans. I can't seem to stop with her. The sound of her voice, the memory of the feeling of my cock in her mouth…

Her voice goes all sensual as she gives a giggle. "Mmm… is that right?"

"Yeah. It was a special night." Fuck. I can't keep my hands off my cock. I unzip my jeans, sliding a hand down over my crotch. "I'd like to see you again."

"The answer is the same as the last time you called. No. I'm sorry. I think you're really great. I had a…" She sighs as she tries to choose her words. "Nice time."

"Nice?" I hold in a groan, my hand moving faster over my shaft. "You call me taking you from the back while you're on your hands and knees in an alleyway…" My balls tighten as I fight to keep the impending climax from my voice. "Nice?"

She starts chatting, offering a steady stream of flirty comments. As she speaks, my mind goes back to that place, the tightness of her pussy, the sound of her moans. The orgasm tightens all my muscles at once. I give a deep groan.

"Wait a minute." Curiosity laces her words.

Oh shit. Was that groan out loud?

"Huh?" I grunt.

I can picture her throwing her hand on her hip as she demands, "Exactly what are you doing right now?"

"Exactly?" I say.

"Yes."

"Taking off my shirt." I slip my shirt up over the back of my neck.

"And why would you be taking off your shirt while you're on the phone with me?"

"To clean the cum off my cock." I wipe up the slippery mess with my tee shirt.

"Are you serious!" she shrieks into the phone. "You..." her words drop to a whisper, *"masturbated...* while you were on the phone with me?"

"Yes. I couldn't help myself. Thinking of my cock in your mouth, my cock in your tight little pussy—"

"You are seriously unbelievable. A total Beast. Goodbye, Nikolaos."

She hangs up the phone. Rejected again. I'm getting used to it.

Doesn't mean I'll give up.

I clean myself up.

I couldn't stop calling her after the dance we shared. And now, I can't stop calling her again. Just to hear her voice. But the calls aren't the main problem. It's been weeks since I last saw her.

I can't stop thinking about her. And the real confusing piece? It's not just the sex I'm caught up on.

It's her laugh. Her eyes. The way she smells.

I'm obsessed.

I have to stop this madness. That will be my last phone call. I'm moving on. Hell, maybe I'll even go out tonight. Pick up a woman. Do something to make me forget Charlie and move on with my life.

Settled. Boys' night out it is.

An hour later, I'm in the city, the other single brothers at my side. I order a round of whiskeys, taking the tray over to the table and passing them out to my friends.

I hold up a glass in cheers to the group. "Thanks for coming out. I needed this." I slide into the seat beside Aiden.

Aiden gives a scoff as he chokes down his whiskey. "No shit. You've been in a funk ever since you went to the Village."

"Yeah. I think it's just work stress. We're trying to pull off something big." I take a sip. "I guess it's taken its toll."

"Work stress? I call bullshit. You were an Air Marshal in the past, a very high stress job you seemed to manage just fine. You haven't had a single issue since you started working for the family. If anything, I'd say you thrive in intense situations." Aiden gives me a hard stare. "I think it's something else that has you messed up."

"Yeah? And what would that be?" I ask.

He raises his brows. "Your funk wouldn't have something to do with a pretty little widow in the family, would it?"

I give a grunt.

He laughs.

"I came here tonight specifically to meet women," I say.

He nods. "Great idea. Have a piece. Indulge in a little distraction. But when the sun comes up and that woman is in your bed, you know who you'll be thinking about. Your flowery little widow." He takes a sip. "Is it really worth the hassle?"

"To get laid?" I shrug. "Maybe."

"Whatever. We need more whiskey." He gives my back a good-natured slap as he gets up to go to the bar for another round.

As if on cue, a tall, beautiful brunette slides into Aiden's open seat. Her eyes sparkle as she turns them on me. "Hey there. I couldn't help but notice you from the other side of the room." She reaches out, resting a hand lightly on my shoulder. "You're just so…" Her gaze travels over the full length of my body, taking a moment to settle on my crotch before making its way back up to my face. "Big."

"Yeah. They make 'em bigger where I come from." I look for Aiden. Where's my whiskey?

Her hand travels from my shoulder over my bicep. I feel like a piece of meat at the butcher that she's eyeing, sizing up, deciding if I'm the cut of meat she wants to take home for dinner.

Charlie would never be so forward. Her cheeks blush just trying to say any word that has to do with sex out loud. I want to laugh, thinking of how she had to whisper the word *masturbated* into the phone last night.

I give the woman a pleasant enough smile. "My friend's waiting for me at the bar. Nice to meet you."

She gives a disappointed pout. "I'll be here all night in case you change your mind."

I grunt noncommittally at her.

I stand at the bar with Aiden, shooting the shit and sipping on whiskey. I don't usually drink. These whiskeys are the first I've had in a year. I think I'm drunk. I call it a night and head home. Crash on my couch, the same one I jacked off on earlier while talking to Charlie. I pick up my phone.

It's after midnight. I want to drunk dial. I want to hear her voice.

She's made it clear—she wants nothing to do with me. I have to move on. I have to stop calling her.

But I want to. I need to.

I pass out trying to decide.

I wake to the ringing of my phone. The sun blinds me as I open my eyes.

"Nikolaos?"

"Yes?"

It's one of my men from the Village. "You told me to call if I heard anything about her, had any news."

"Yeah?" I sit up, rubbing the whiskey-induced sleep from my eyes. "What have you heard?"

"Are you sitting down?"

"Yes." What's he on about? "Why?"

"Because what I'm about to tell you is going to change your world."

CHAPTER
FIVE

Charlie

A chill creeps up my spine, like something bad is about to happen. Those little hairs stand up on the back of my neck. My gut tells me to call the girls and cancel, to not go out tonight, that this girls' night out is a bad idea.

Am I being silly? No. I'm not crazy—I'm cursed. My life's track record speaks for itself.

"Come on, Charlie. Everything is fine." I smooth a hand over my hair, taking in my reflection in the antique Queen Anne mirror, its wide frame leafed in gold.

I touch the cool strand of pearls at my neck. I turn a toe to reveal the red bottom of my heel, a reminder of who I've become. I've gone with the *Me Dolly* black suede slide, the heel high enough to count but still comfy enough to stroll around the city without turning an ankle or, God forbid, having ankles swell into cankles.

Hair fresh from the stylist, my signature light ash brown gloss covering my natural blonde, perfectly curled with not a strand out of place. Not a wrinkle in my favorite dress, the big pink flowers so bright and cheerful they almost make me smile.

I grab the bottle of Chanel Coco Mademoiselle, a gift from Emilia when she left New York and went back to her home in Italy. I spray a spritz in the air and breeze through it, letting the light, floral perfume envelop me. I set the bottle down on the dressing table, glancing at my reflection. A bright, perfectly glossed smile flashes back at me in the mirror.

I look good. Normal. Like me. Charlie Bachman.

Loved, wanted, undamaged.

I look like I'm ready for a night out with the Beauties. No one will ever know I've spent the past seven days wearing sweats, my hair swept up in a messy bun, my old bunny slippers looking more bedraggled than ever, red rims lining my eyes.

So why do I still feel so empty inside?

My hand circles my belly.

I've been thinking about my childhood way too much. I hate how when you're low your brain takes you even lower, making you dwell on bad memories. My hand leaves my stomach, my forced smile curling up to the blushed apples of my cheeks.

Remember who you are, not who you were. Charlie Bachman. A strong, beautiful, caring woman with a huge chosen family and more girlfriends than I could have ever imagined I'd have.

Right now I should be in serious need of some girl-time.

I shake my head as if the movement will empty the thoughts from my brain.

"There's no use thinking sad thoughts, Charlie. Time to move on." My eyes are not convincing me, and my teeth sink into my bottom lip. I straighten my spine and steady my gaze, telling my reflection, "Tonight is supposed to be *fun*."

I go down to my kitchen, needing to feed my fish before I leave. I give my blue and red beta a few flakes of food. He darts out of his pirate ship, coming to the surface to gulp them down, his pretty, fanned-out tail flicking happily. "See you later, Captain Jack Sparrow."

He's the only man I've come home to for the past five years.

The pendulum wall clock strikes eight, Westminster chiming through my New York townhouse. It's time. I can practically hear the champagne-laced giggles, the clacking of the herd of stilettos headed toward my house. A few off-key peals of "Rock the Boat" catch my ear. Has to be Shannon. My doorbell starts chiming and it doesn't stop.

"Coming! Coming!" I call, rushing down the stairs as quickly as I can without turning an ankle in my too-high girls' night out heels. "Hang on!"

I throw the door open, and I'm instantly enveloped in a cloud of hugs and perfume and colorful fabrics. My mood lightens as Shannon hooks her arm through mine. "You're looking grand! Love the dress. You look like a garden in bloom."

Everyone else wears sleek cocktail dresses. I'm feeling a bit out of place in my flouncy floral number.

"Thanks." I twist the gold bracelet on my wrist, suddenly nervous tonight is a mistake, that I'm not ready to go out, and that what I really need is another quiet night in by myself, tearing through an entire box of Kleenex while ingesting a whole pyramid of Ferrero Rochers.

But I'm here now and there's no call to be rude or a quiet little mouse sulking in the corner. After all, this night was put together for me. My friends noticed I'd been a little blue and wanted to cheer me up.

I push myself to be a good friend back, asking about Shannon's upcoming honeymoon. "So are you and Mark counting down the days till you get to leave this winter behind for paradise?"

Shannon and her husband were married just a few weeks ago. She was ready to hit the white sand beaches of the Cayman Islands the moment she said I do, but her husband Mark wanted to spend a few weeks in their new townhome to get settled before they left for their two-week vacation.

Her eyes light up like Christmas trees. "I. Can. Not. Wait. It's gonna be crackin'!" She launches into an excited monologue listing all the activities they'll be doing, punctuating it with her adorable Irish slang. Unlike me, she and Mark are both adventure bugs and adrenaline junkies. Skydiving, zip-lining, snorkeling, diving, swimming with dolphins.

I've been to the Caymans before. Once. It didn't end well for me. The memory creeps up in my mind. I take a deep breath, pushing it down, reminding myself Shannon's not cursed.

Just me.

"You're going to have an amazing time," I say, stretching my smile a little too wide.

Tess threads her arm through my other arm, giving me a squeeze and an understanding glance. "Yes. Everything will be perfect." She knows what I've been through. "Now let's get this party started!"

Shannon gives an excited, "Whoot! Whoot!"

The two gorgeous redheads bookend me and we make our way down the street to where the cars wait for us. The girls both look so stunning in their sleek black gowns, I feel a bit like the double-stuffed cream in the middle of this sleek girl-cookie sandwich.

Three packed Escalades and a short drive later, we're spilling out onto the sidewalk in front of Angels and Devils, New York's hottest club at the moment. Our large group of dolled-up, giggling women cruises into the black lacquer-walled room, strutting across the gleaming red flooring.

I look up, taking in the entertainment.

Beautiful women in sparkling leotards hang from the ceiling, balancing in giant lit-up circles, contorting their bodies in all kinds of impossible poses while managing to keep the massive, shimmering white wings that hang on their backs untangled.

Shirtless men with oiled chests strut through the room, handsome devils offering bottle service from their trays. Horns are perched on their heads, translucent black glass lit by what looks like a real flame from inside. When they move, the points at the ends of their devils' tails swish behind them.

Sultry music pipes through the club, couples pairing off to grind on the dance floor to a slow number. I take the shot glass Tess hands me. A flame burns from the top of the glass, rich liquor fills the bottom.

"Blow it out before you drink it. It's called a Flaming Amy." She purses her bloodred lips, blowing out her flame and tossing back her shot.

"Thanks for the tip," I laugh, wondering if I've really been that out of it lately that she feels the need to tell me to blow out a burning shot before I drink it. I tip the warmed liquor down my throat. It's sickly sweet and makes my stomach turn.

"Another one!" she shouts, throwing her head back and pumping her fist in the air. The Beauties surround her, passing around colorful shot glasses. I take one, knowing they'll pressure me like schoolgirls if I try to turn it down.

This night is for me. I know that. And I love them for it.

I'm just not… feeling it. I long for the quiet poolside of Liam's Italian country estate, a good book, and one of Marta's famous cinnamon rolls to end the night. The girls chant a countdown to take their shots. "Three… two… one!" As they tip back their liquor, I take the opportunity to tip mine over into the trash can.

The music changes, the thump of the bass rattling my head. Tess puts a light hand on my shoulder. "Whew! That was strong!"

I make a face. "Yeah. Boy, that was strong one."

She waggles her brows, already looking a little tipsy. "Whew! I feel warm and tingly all over. Rockland's going to be a lucky man tonight! Come on!"

She grabs my hand, pulling me toward the throng of pulsing bodies. As the red flooring changes to the sleek wood dance floor, my heel snags on something, making me trip forward. Tess's strong grip on my arm is the only thing that keeps me from hitting the floor.

"Whoa, girl!" She laughs. "Those shots must have gone to your head."

"No. My shoe caught on something—" But Tess is already dancing, pumping her hips between Shannon and Hannah. I stand there, swaying to the music, but I just can't get into it.

A drunk woman in a lime green dress who looks like she's not a day over nineteen bumps into me. I watch in horror as the pink liquid from her glass comes flying at me. It's like slow motion. I have no time to react and now I'm covered in the sticky drink.

"Oh my gawd! I'm *sooo* sorry. Like, so sorry." She puts a chipped fingernail to her over-glossed lips, giggling.

"It's fine, don't worry about it." I try to smile but tears burn in the corners of my eyes. I push past her, heading to the bathroom.

The restroom attendant—a woman in a black and red gown—sees me coming and hands me a fluffy white towel. "Here you go, honey. Let me know if I can help."

"Thanks." I dab at the dress but it's no use, the fabric has already absorbed the liquid and I'm left with a pink splotch in the center of my chest, reeking of rum.

I toss the towel on the counter, staring back at myself in the mirror. "This is not your night."

Scratch that. This is not my month. Maybe not my lifetime. If I believed in reincarnation, I'd be trying to find some good luck spell to put on myself for the next time around the block.

I can't stop my hand from going to my belly. An ache tears through me as I smooth down my dress. I just want to go home, take a shower, put on some cozy pajamas, pop a frozen barbecue chicken pizza in the oven and turn on a cheesy rom-com.

I seriously cannot handle one more thing going wrong tonight…

I leave the restroom, ready to make my excuses to the girls. They'll be disappointed but they'll understand. I'll send flowers and a handwritten note to each of them in the morning, thanking them for the thoughtful evening and apologizing for leaving early.

I'm so deep in thought, I'm the one who bumps into someone this time, luckily with no drink in my hand.

"Oh, excuse me!" I steady myself, having run into the broad wall of a man's muscular chest.

Strong hands grab my shoulders, steadying me. "Careful there."

"Oh…" I freeze. Instantly I recognize the deep timbre, the slight lilt at the end of the word, the husky Greek accent. "Hello."

I look up into the dark eyes of the Beast. Our gazes lock and for the second time tonight, time slows. What on earth is *he* doing here? He offers no greeting back. Just stares.

"So, um, how have you been? I haven't seen you since the…" Blowjob in the alleyway? "Winter Ball. That was what? Three months ago?" As ridiculous as it is to try to make small talk with him, I can't not. It's in my nature.

He just keeps staring. My bad mood returns. He could make an effort. At least say something. Why is he even here tonight? I didn't take him for a club goer.

Finally, even I can't play polite anymore. My hands go to my hips, and I demand, "What? Why are you staring at me?"

That voice, low and even but demanding at its edges, caresses me as he speaks. "Don't you have something you need to tell me?"

He… knows…

Trickles of ice travel up my spine and along my hairline.

How?

Only two people in this world know my secret. And one of us is dead.

What do I do? Tell him the truth? Ask what he's heard?

I stare back at him. My tongue goes to move but it grows thick in my mouth. The tears that seem to come so easily these days spring up in my eyes. I cannot, will not, cry in front of him. I have to leave.

Now.

I clear my tightening throat. "No," I manage, my voice shaking. "I don't." I turn on my heel, my hair swinging over my shoulder as I go back to my group.

The heat of his stare burns the skin at the back of my neck.

CHAPTER SIX

Beast

I'm going to make her tell me the truth. She owes me that much. How she's kept her secret this long, I don't understand.

As she passes by me, the scent of rum reaches my nose. Has she been drinking? In her condition? In two long strides I'm over to her. I grab her arm, stopping her. "Hold on. I'm not finished talking to you."

She tugs her arm from my grasp. "Well, I'm done talking to you."

Crossing her arms over her chest, she stares daggers at me. Her eyes are steely, but they have a sheen of tears in them.

"What's wrong?" I ask.

"Nothing," she says, her voice cracking. "Everything." She shakes her head. "I don't know."

I stand in shock as Charlie Bachman crumbles in front of me. The woman who's never made an appearance with a hair out of place and a smile always plastered on her face is now curling into herself, shakily dabbing at the tears that are threatening to fall down her cheeks.

And I have absolutely no idea what to do. My anger toward her melts. I want to get to the bottom of what I've been told, I want to find out the truth.

But right now...

"You want to get out of here?" I wrap an arm around her shoulders.

She gives a sniffle and a nod. "Yes, please."

I guide her out of the club.

"What are you even doing here tonight?" She looks up at me, her eyes shining.

"Looking for you."

A pretty flush patches over her cheeks. "Oh."

"Yeah."

Her voice trembles. "So, you heard."

"Yes."

"How?" she asks.

I shrug. "Rumor mill." I leave it at that.

I can't seem to stop obsessing over the woman.

She shakes her head. "Dr. Thompson was the only one who knew besides me. And he's gone now. I really don't know how anyone else knew."

"May he rest in peace."

Dr. Thompson died peacefully in his sleep a few weeks ago. I don't come all the way clean, telling her I've been keeping close tabs on her ever since the alleyway. That I got a phone call after the beloved doctor died. That one of my men found the results of a pregnancy test he gave in his office a few weeks before he died. It was Charlie's, and it was positive. I knew instantly the baby was mine.

"Yes. He was a good man. Discreet. Or at least, so I thought." She eyes me, trying to see if she can get me to spill my source. I'm a locked box. Sighing, she looks away. "Well, I don't know how you know, but I'm sorry to tell you—"

"Why didn't you tell me right away?" I interrupt.

My gruffness brings the tears back to her eyes. Her voice is a whisper. "There was nothing to tell."

When she looks up at me, it's with such utter heartache, I can't speak for a moment, my tongue going numb in my mouth. She's hurting. Really hurting. I've got to find out what's going on with her.

"Come with me." I grab her hand, ignoring the electricity I feel when our skin touches. My driver waits at the back door of my Suburban. Wordlessly he greets us, holding the door open. "Get in," I say.

"Thank you." She looks grateful as she enters the warm cab, sliding across the leather bench seat.

I get in, closing the door. My driver asks, "Where to?"

I say, "Her house." I grab a tissue from the stocked armrest, handing it to her. She thanks me again, dabbing at the corners of her eyes. Turning my body toward hers, I wait for her to speak.

"There really isn't much to tell…" Her quiet tears turn to little sobs.

The sound tears at my chest. I reach out, putting a heavy hand on her knee. "Take your time."

"A few weeks after our... um..."

"After we had sex," I offer. I'm trying to be sensitive here, but I can't help that flicker of my cock at the memory...

Her words come out shaky and fast. "Yes, about eight weeks after we had sex, I noticed I missed my period. I didn't think too much of it because my cycle is kind of long anyway and I'd been busy with the holidays and charities and such and sometimes when I get really stressed, I miss it. But then, about a week later I ordered fish tacos but when they came to the table I got this queasy feeling, so I took a test."

"A pregnancy test."

"Yes. A pregnancy test. It wasn't a math test," she adds with a touch of snark. "But there was a plus sign."

I'm confused. She seems like someone who would be excited to be pregnant. "Plus is good, right?"

"Depends on the person." Her voice goes soft and her gaze trails from my face to the window, staring out at the city as it goes by. As if without thinking about it, her hand goes to her stomach. "For me, it wasn't good."

My chest sinks a bit. Stupid, I know, but it hurts, her not wanting our baby.

She turns back to me, finishing her thought. "It was great. Amazing. A miracle, really."

"So, you were... happy?"

"Yes. Thrilled. Over the moon." But her face is so sad. There's more to this story. "I didn't tell a soul, I was so, so overjoyed, I just couldn't believe it was true. I had to see for myself before I shared the news, and of course you would have been first. I went to see Dr. Thompson for an appointment right away. I wanted to use our family doctor. I thought... I thought of you, and that you would want me to go to him."

"It's true. Thank you."

"You don't have to thank me." She waves a shaky hand through the air. "Because it didn't matter in the end. Any of it."

"Tell me. What happened?"

"He told me he was going to do an internal ultrasound. Before he started, I had him reassure me twice that he would be able to print out something for me to share with you. He said at this point in the pregnancy the baby would just be a cute little teddy graham, but he would have pics to send home with me." She folds her hands in her lap. "I had this whole idea of how to tell you. I was going to make a little card, tape the ultrasound picture inside and write, Little Baby Beast. Silly, I know. The two of us barely even know one another..."

Guilt flows over me, hot and cringey. I hunted the poor girl down tonight to tear her secrets from her. "So you were going to tell me?"

"Yes. Right away. My plan was to go to your place and give you the card as soon as I left his office. I kept picturing your face when I told you. I had no idea how you'd react. I mean, I know we didn't know one another that well"—her face heats— "I mean, other than being intimate, but I wouldn't hold a secret like that from you. Not for a second. You have the right to know. But Oh. My. Gosh. Can I tell you how nervous I was to tell you? I kept trying to picture your stoic face when you read the note."

How would I have reacted? I have absolutely no idea. I've never been in this position before. When I'd first heard that she was pregnant, I'll admit, I went numb. Being a father isn't something I'd ever considered.

I want to know more. "Keep going."

A little breath shudders through her chest as she steels her nerves to go on. "I just laid there as still as could be, waiting to hear the heartbeat. He said that we would hear it, that there would be this precious little swish-swish noise that would change my life forever. But then, I could tell it was taking longer than it should. The screen was just dark with white circles and patches. I couldn't tell what I was looking at. Dr. Thompson got this frown on his face, and I could just tell, something was wrong..." Her voice breaks and she has to stop.

"Take your time," I say, stroking her thigh.

She takes a little breath, gathering her courage. Her eyes meet mine. The rawness of the emotion there is almost too much but I don't look away. I want to bear this pain with her. She continues, her voice shaky. "He pointed to the screen. There were two little circles, a smaller one inside of a larger one. A yolk and a sac, he said. But no baby."

Positive pregnancy test but no baby in her belly? "How can that be?"

She shakes her head. "It's just something that happens. He explained it to me, and then of course, I went home and did hours of Google research over it. It's called a blighted ovum. The pregnancy forms to the point of creating hormones in your body, the yolk and the sac like I could see on the screen, tricking your body into thinking it's pregnant. The early embryo stops developing or never develops at all, leaving an empty gestational sac. You have enough hormones in your urine or bloodstream to get a positive pregnancy test, sometimes even enough to feel sick or nauseous, but... there's just no baby."

What do I say? Heat creeps up the back of my neck. I'm not good with this kind of stuff, feelings, emotions, babies. But I know she's hurting. "That must have been...terrible. And to face it alone..."

She nods, looking a bit relieved that I somewhat understand. "It was. I was shocked. And crushed. And I know it's completely irrational, but I just felt so silly, so humiliated, that I thought I was pregnant when I wasn't."

"It's not your fault."

"I know. Irrational, like I said, still. I just felt so... embarrassed. Especially because I was so excited. I wasn't in my right mind. I even made him make an appointment to see me the following week. I didn't want to do anything until I was 100% sure there was no baby. He respected my request. I spent a week pacing the floors of my house, praying for a miracle, but I knew as soon as I stepped into his office I was going to put myself through hell all over again. Sure enough, nothing had changed. I just left more brokenhearted than before."

I run a hand through my hair. "Jesus, that's rough. And no one knew what you went through?"

"No." She bites her lip. "I didn't want them to. I just felt so sad and... ashamed. Which, again, I knew was crazy, but I couldn't stop feeling that way." Her pretty hazel eyes find mine. "I'm sorry I didn't tell you. I thought about it, you know. Even if there was no baby, I figured you had a right to know there could have been one, if that makes sense, but every time I thought about telling you, I would just start crying and I couldn't bear the thought of breaking down in front of you."

She's tearing up now.

"Don't cry." I don't know what to say. She looks so sad, so broken. She said no one knew except for the doctor. Has she been dealing with this all on her own? "What happened then?"

She shrugs. "He gave me some medicine to help... it... pass. I took it at home, spent a day in agony, then seven more in pajamas, crying on my sofa. My friends knew I was down, but they didn't know why. They organized this night out to cheer me up, but I'm still under a dark cloud, I guess." Her voice goes to such a low whisper I barely hear what she says next. "I wanted that baby so very badly."

Her words make the hairs on the back of my neck stand on end. There's so much emotion in her voice, chills run down my spine. I clear my throat. "Have you been back to the doctor to make sure everything is okay?"

"I had a follow-up scheduled but I couldn't. He died!" The color drains from her face. "And I got this terrible feeling his death had something to do with me. Silly, I know, but I haven't had the guts to find a new doctor."

She needs to be seen by someone. As soon as possible. I don't know how these things work but I know that after something like what she's been through, a follow-up visit must be important.

We pull up to her robin's egg blue door. Matching planters sit on either side of the door, holding perfectly pruned topiaries. A cheerful wreath adorns her door. Picture perfect.

She's anything but. Her face is pale, her eyes red, her spirit waning.

I can't let her go in there alone. She shouldn't be alone. She's a strong woman but after what she's been through... everything I put her through. I got her pregnant and caused her all of this suffering. It's my responsibility to make sure she's well.

"Driver. Take us to my house."

Charlie gives me a curious look, opening her lips to protest.

"Now."

CHAPTER
SEVEN

Charlie

Where are we? We've been driving for hours. The lightless night sky is so dark you can actually see the stars out here. I'd say it's beautiful but the further I get from civilization, alone with this man I barely know, the more eerie my surroundings feel.

The Suburban climbs the steep gravel road, winding through the dense forest of trees. My Vera Bradley blue paisley overnight bag sits between me and the Beast. After telling the driver to go to his house, I at least convinced him to let me pop into my house first. I texted the girls so they wouldn't worry and changed into comfy yoga pants and Ugg boots, then he gave me a total of five minutes to pack. I threw my beauty care routine, a few other toiletries, and some comfy clothes in the bag, then nestled it between us as a safety measure.

I have no idea where we are going or how long he is keeping me. This is crazy... He's basically kidnapping me.

And for what? To be sure I'm healthy after *not* having his baby that wasn't even really a baby?

This is so messed up. I never, ever should have put my nose where it didn't belong. I never should have gone down to the alleyway that night. My life has been an absolute disaster ever since. I've gone from facing bitter loneliness to now feeling utter and total devastation as well.

For the hundred-and-tenth time since we left my house, I say, "This really isn't necessary."

For the hundred-and-tenth time, he replies with a grunt-like sound, daring me to argue.

The Suburban pulls into a little grove of trees. I slide to the middle of the seat, peering out through the windshield. Water, black ripples of water, moonlight shining down, casting a glowing white light on their shimmering peaks. It must be a lake.

"Where are we going?" I ask again, knowing I won't get the answer I'm looking for.

He simply grabs my bag and exits the car, holding the door open for me like a perfect gentleman.

He's anything but.

The tenderness from the car ride has dissipated. I'm so confused by this transition to hardness after what felt like understanding. He goes back and forth with every breath I take, now holding out his hand. I take it, needing it to steady me as I hop down from the high car.

"Thank you."

I get another grunt.

I stare out over the lake. It's gorgeous. Vast and moonlit, surrounded by trees. In the middle of the lake there's another landform, its surface covered in tall, thick evergreens. An island?

He walks ahead of me, his strides long, and I have to almost jog to keep up with him. My boots crunch over gravel as I speak. "Where are we going?"

He lifts a huge hand, pointing to the island. "There."

"Well, I guessed as much, but what *is* over there?" A cold breeze rustles my hair, leaving the tiny hairs on the back of my neck and my arms standing on end. Where is he taking me? What if he's some kind of serial killer or something and what's waiting for me out on that lake is a moldy dungeon...

"They call it Dark Island," he says.

The trees are so thick, the landscape is almost black. "I can see why."

"It's my home, the island."

"Your home?" I squeak.

Oh gosh, please do not tell me he's enrolled me in some get-better-wilderness-retreat out here in the woods. This girl might love flowers but when it comes to roughing it in nature, I have two words for you.

Unh-uh.

"Umm... This isn't like a camping thing, is it?" I ask.

He glances back at me, his brows knit together in confusion. "Camping?"

"You said your home is the island. I'm just wondering if it's some kind of outdoorsy—"

"My home is on the island." He gives a scoff of a laugh. "And most wouldn't think the word 'home' does it justice."

The trees start to thin as we reach the shore. There's a pleasant looking motorboat waiting for us, yellow lights glowing over its bow.

I watch my step as we walk toward the shore, grateful for his hand. "Why would most not call it a home?"

For the first time tonight, he gives me what looks like a genuine smile. "You'll see." His straight white teeth shine in the moonlight, his eyes lighting from within, and I feel his grin down in my belly.

He's insanely handsome when he smiles like that.

"You should smile more often," I whisper to myself more than to him, but he must hear me because my comment receives a grunt. I didn't mean to be rude. Change of subject. He must love his home if it makes him smile like that. "You must like it here."

"I do. It's quiet."

Quiet. Like him. I don't think the man said more than ten words on our drive, even when I poured my heart out to him about the pregnancy. He reached for my hand, I guess showing support in his own way, but he's definitely a man of few words.

It makes me wonder how this stay will go. I picture his home as a small, rustic cabin, one or two bedrooms, the two of us staring across a table at one another, sipping on some soup he's concocted of wild game he came across on the island.

Yeah, it's going to be awkward with a capital A.

Why did I even agree to come?

Wait—I didn't ever agree to come, did I? He forced me to be here, against my will. I should run, scream, tell his driver or whoever is captain of this boat to take me home. I should demand to be taken back to the city.

The thought of my empty townhome, the discarded boxes of tissues, the silly rom-coms playing endlessly on the TV, the well-meaning Beauties who drop by for visits but who I have nothing to say to right now, makes my heart sink. I guess this won't be so bad, to get away for a while.

Even if this is how every single murder scene in a movie starts out… strange man isolating a woman in the woods. I stare out over the water at the thick trees, and something about the dark surface makes my mind flash to the ultrasound, to the emptiness. I don't want to be home. Or alone. And I could really use some quiet.

I'll take my chances.

It's not like I have a choice anyway. He's made up his mind. I sneak a glance at my companion as he makes his way down to the boat, his shoulders brimming with determination. I prepare myself for one-sided conversations that end with a grunt.

Aiden, the man driving the boat, is younger than us, a brother. I can tell by the black circle tattoo that peeks out over the undone top buttons of his shirt. Nikolaos has one too. I've caught glimpses. The driver's greeting to me is nothing more than a nod. I sink down into one of the two leather captain's chairs and we're off.

The motor is a soft hum, the quiet night pierced only by a few even-pitched trills of what I can only guess is an owl. The water laps at the sides of the boat, a soothing sound that would relax me if I wasn't so keyed up.

What on earth am I doing right now? The boat pulls up to a dock and Aiden keeps the engine running.

"All good?" Beast asks Aiden.

"Yep." Aiden glances over his shoulder, looking over the mainland. "One and done for the night."

Beast gives a nod. "Good. Very good." He grabs my bag, hopping over the edge of the boat onto the dock in a surprisingly graceful move for such a large man.

I wait for him to offer me his hand, knowing he will before he even does. I take it, and there's that energy there as our skin meets. I follow him off the dock onto the pebbled trail that leads into the dark woods. There're little solar lights illuminating each side of the path but it's not enough to ease the eeriness that comes from walking through the woods in the dark.

"I really can see why they call it Dark Island," I say, trying not to look as spooked as I feel. Another owl hoots and I almost jump out of my skin.

His hold tightens around my hand. "It's peaceful, though. Isn't it?"

"Peaceful in a spooky sort of Halloween way, I guess." A stick cracks under my footstep and I jump again. "I'm not a nature lover."

"Really? You could have fooled me with those dresses. You look like a walking garden half the time."

"I love organized nature," I say, stressing the word organized. "Gardens, flower bouquets, those kinds of things. Oh, and yes, I have a soft spot for floral prints."

He side-eyes me. "I prefer you in the sweats."

I laugh, tugging at the hem of my sweatshirt. "Well, this is the real me, messy ponytail and all."

He openly stares at me for a moment as we walk. "You look great to me."

Whoa, was that a compliment from the Beast?

I clear my throat, trying to cool the heat creeping up my cheeks. "Hmm." I don't know what to say but I leave my hand in his, confused by how safe I feel at his side and yet how I'm still a bit terrified of him. The woods start to thin.

His house comes into view.

Only, it's not a house.

It's a freaking castle.

"Oh. My. Goodness." I stop and just stand there, taking it all in. *"This* is your... *house?"*

He stares up at the castle, a light of pride in his handsome face. "Home sweet home."

"And what a home it is..." My words trail off as my mind tries to accept the fact that this place is real.

The granite structure is softly lit with fire-like sconces on either side of the door, beams of soft light shooting up from the ground, making shadows along the stone walls. Several large, arched windows are lit from within, a warm, welcoming glow shining from their panes. The building is massive, with towers and turrets.

A real castle.

He recounts the history of the place. Dozens of Italian stonemasons shaped the granite for the red-tile-roofed, four-story, thirty-room castle and the four-story tower, as well as for a large boathouse on the shore. There's even a two-story icehouse that was used like a giant refrigerator for fine dining ingredients at the turn of the previous century. Over two thousand loads of topsoil were brought from Canada to cover the ten acres of rocky soil, hence the lush grass growing beneath our feet. The castle is complete with all the things you'd expect from a legit castle: secret tunnels, scullery kitchens, gardens, more turrets. He tells me there's even a dungeon and underground passageways.

"What have you done with the dungeon?" I ask, a shiver moving down my spine as the breeze whips through my hair. The shiver turns to sensual chills as he turns to me, the open lust in his gaze heating my face.

He runs the tip of his tongue over his lips in a way that makes me think of Kylie and Cannon's sex club, Fire, and all the sexy rooms set up there for playtime. His husky voice drops an octave as he says, "Maybe I'll show you sometime."

His reaction makes me certain. He's turned the dungeon into a sex room.

What is he doing out here on this island? I mean, joining the family comes with money, but last I heard, he was only overseeing security at the Hamlet, the family's town in Connecticut where not much ever happens.

I'm curious. "How are you able to live all the way out here? Shouldn't you be at the Hamlet?"

"I have excellent staff. I keep in contact with them whenever I'm here."

It still begs the question, what kind of operation is he running here for the family? Obviously, there's more going on than off-site security. It'd be rude to ask these questions and it just isn't in my nature to be rude. I bite my tongue.

"You're welcome anywhere in the castle." It's an invitation, but he says it in a foreboding manner.

Just the castle? "What about the rest of the island?" I ask.

"You're welcome anywhere in the castle," he repeats, giving me a look that says he will not be repeating himself often.

Whew, the heat that comes off of that tense jawline when he's admonishing me. Kinda makes me a little weak in the knees and tickly in the tummy. The man is in command and in control. Seeing the way he carries himself on his own property just heightens the natural weight of leadership he already carries on his massive shoulders.

A hot man who owns and runs his own island and lives in a castle? Not gonna lie. It's a huge turn-on. And his taste, goodness, I've never seen a bachelor deck out a house like this.

Maybe I shouldn't have been turning him down during all those phone calls he made to me.

We walk up the stone steps. A staff member opens the massive oak doors for us. My breath catches in my throat as I step over the threshold into the grand foyer of the castle. There's nothing gothic or creepy about it. It's one of the most beautiful spaces I've ever been in.

I arch my neck, staring up at the three stories of open tower that soar above our heads, arched windows letting out the warm golden light I first saw when I stood in the front yard. The ceiling is made of stained planks of wood, trimmed into triangles and meeting in a point at the interior top of the tower.

Under my feet, the white marble flooring is inlaid with a red diamond pattern that forms a star bursting out from the center of the room. Gold and glass tables sit on the perimeter of the circular room, their edges curved to follow the rounded walls. Thin branches with green leaves and fresh white Popcorn Viburnum, living up to their name with their fluffy white flowers, stand in tall glass vases.

He leads me deeper into the castle. I'm surprised by how warm the lighting is, how tastefully the place is decorated. Thick Persian carpets in warm reds and golds and blues. Gold chandeliers and sconce lighting, but they're not ornate, just simple in their beauty.

We enter a large room; its stucco walls are painted a soft dove gray, and dark wood beams stretch out across the entirety of the white ceiling overhead, placed every few feet. Multiple couches are arranged around the room, their fabric deep reds and blues. They look so soft I'd want to collapse into one if I wasn't so keyed up. The largest stone fireplace I've ever seen sits at one end of the room, boasting a roaring wood-burning fire, the cozy sound of wood crackling filling the room. The mantel is a long, gorgeous piece of polished wood, taken from a tree on the island, I assume. Its edge follows the natural grain in the wood, curving in and out.

"My favorite room," he says.

"I can see why. It's beautiful."

He seems to like my approval, and a little tension leaves his shoulders as he watches my face as I admire the place.

The back wall of the room is all glass rectangular doors outlined in black metal. He flips a switch on the wall and the backyard lights up. He flicks another and, like magic, the doors start to ease to the right, folding into one another.

"You're welcome out here anytime. Just stay close to the castle." We step out onto a gorgeous stone veranda overlooking the lake.

The yard is manicured, each blade of green grass standing perfectly at attention. He's got a full outdoor kitchen, a gas fireplace, a movie screen, and plenty of outdoor seating that looks sleek but cozy. Stone pavers circle a lit, in-ground pool complete with hot tub and a little waterfall flowing from the edge of its wall back down into the pool. Steam rises from the blue-lit water, calling me into its warm depths.

"One more thing." He gestures to the right.

"Huh?" It takes a moment for me to close my dropped jaw and tear my gaze away from the backyard to see what he's pointing at. In the dark night I can barely see the small stone cottage sitting by the lakeshore in the distance. "What's the one thing?"

His dark eyes hold mine. "Never, ever step foot in the boathouse."

"Well, that sounds ominous enough."

I'm reminded of the off-limits west wing of the Disney version of the Beast's castle and my imagination wanders. Is he hiding a rose, trying to break a curse as each petal falls? My goodness, will there be a singing teapot at my disposal? I can't stop the giggle that bursts forth from my mouth then somehow finds its way into my nose. My hand covers my face, but the unattractive snort still escapes.

He gives me a look crossed somewhere between amusement and annoyance.

I have to ask. "What's in the boathouse?"

The look turns to a steely gaze of warning.

"Doesn't matter, does it? Just stay away." With that he turns on his bootheel, leading me back into the house. "Oh, yeah. And I forgot to tell you. There's no internet and no cell reception on this island. Your phone is useless here. I'll get in touch with the family and let them know you're on an extended vacation."

Umm.... He just told me I have no contact with the outside world while I'm here. And no access to online shopping and my obsessive Pinterest boards either. "No phone? No internet?" I rush to catch up with him.

Just a few hours ago, I was ready to leave the club and go back to my townhouse. Lonely, yes, but safe. Very safe. Now I'm here. With him. The boathouse is off-limits. No way to call anyone. The only way off this island is by boat.

How on earth did this happen?

CHAPTER
EIGHT

Beast

It's going to be tough, working with her here. I've kept the family secret this long though; I won't let my impromptu houseguest ruin it now. She'll just have to behave or have that nosy streak whipped right out of her with my belt.

I have a full staff here. Chef Remy I stole from a little French bistro in uptown. My head of housekeeping is a twenty-five-year-old firecracker who runs the house like a woman who's been doing this for decades. Five housekeepers, seven groundskeepers, and a slew of boat crew that rotate day and night shifts.

Day shift for the needs my staff and I have for getting on and off the island. Night shift for bringing my precious cargo onto the island under the cover of darkness. Sounds dramatic, but no one, not one person outside of a very small circle of men, can know what it is we do here on Dark Island.

I introduce Charlie to my key staff, leaving her in their very capable hands to be toured around the castle and settled into her room.

This house has seventeen guest rooms and I made sure she'll be put up in the one next to mine.

Back to work. I head over to the boathouse to check my shipment. Everything is in order. My loyal, determined staff is busy sorting and caring for the delicate cargo under my supervision. An hour later, I leave the boathouse, locking it behind me with the keypad.

I can't stop thinking of Charlie. The way she jumps every time I enter the room, like I'm going to take a big bite out of her, but then runs the tip of that sexy little pink tongue of hers over her lips like *she* wants to take a bite out of *me*.

Doesn't matter if she likes me or not, if she's scared of me or not. She's not leaving this island until the doctor has done a full exam on her. Dr. Williams will be here tomorrow.

The doctor is a friend of mine, a gynecological specialist from the city, tops in her area of expertise, which is researching fertility issues. She's kind, smart, and her easy-going personality seems like a good fit for Charlie. Yes, I chose a woman on purpose. No man other than me will get the pleasure of laying eyes on her beautiful pussy as long as I'm in control.

And right now, I'm completely in control over her. She doesn't leave until I say. It's been made clear to the staff that every single one of her desires and wishes should be met, preemptively, if possible.

All desires save for leaving my island.

Unfortunately, my desire is to fuck her. Hard. From the back. Her on top. In the shower. On the dock. In the pool. In. My. Bed. Christen my bed, really, because I've never, ever had a woman here since I bought this place.

I've been too damn busy. And to be honest... no one compares to Charlie, do they?

Her sweet innocence, covered with a tough exterior, ready to handle whatever the world throws at her with pretty pink nails, perfect curls, flowery dresses, and pouty glossed lips, offering a tray of fresh-baked chocolate chip cookies to whoever she meets.

I called her on numerous occasions, both after the time we danced together and our alleyway rendezvous. I asked her out, several times. She turned me down, every time.

Now she's here.

At my house.

In my care.

With absolutely no way off this island unless I say so.

I'll get her checked out, make sure she's okay, then send her on her way so I can focus on the work I'm doing for the family. Get back to my life.

That's what I should do…

What I *want* is to tear those sweats off her pretty legs. Bury my cock in her. And impregnate her.

Yeah… there's that. I'm not going to unpack that now, but now that I know it's happened once, God, the thought of her pretty belly round, this time healthy and filled with my child… It does something to me, makes my cock throb but also makes this strange fire burn in my chest. Like I said.

Not going to unpack that.

I can't deny the fact I'm getting a fucking kick out of the fact that *the* Charlie Bachman is isolated on my island, completely powerless and under my thumb.

I'll keep her as my guest. And I'll behave.

For now.

CHAPTER NINE

Charlie

I wake to hazelnut and chocolate-filled crepes, powdered sugar melting on their tops, a bowl of fresh fruit next to the plate, and what looks like a latte filling a wide white mug, steam rising from its foam.

The very tall, thin, chipper, ginger-haired chef I remember being introduced to last night leaves me with a grin and a cheerful, "Bon appetit!"

"Thank you so much, Remy!" Remy, just like the chef rat from the kids' movie, *Ratatouille*. "This looks amazing."

I stretch my arms in the air, holding back a yawn. I give him a wave as he leaves the room. He's not an enchanted candlestick or a talking mouse, but the man is magic. The first bite melts in my mouth, the sweet creaminess making me moan.

A short, curvy blonde comes to take the tray away. The Beast has so many staff members I tried to come up with a trick to remember each of their names. I remember her name is Ashely because of her ash-blonde hair, the same shade as my natural hair color before I became a brunette.

"Hey there, sleeping beauty!" She leans the tray against her cocked hip, her wide eyes focusing on me. "Did you have a good night?"

"Slept like a baby—like a rock," I correct myself. How would I know how babies sleep? I pat the mattress beneath me. "This bed is so comfy."

Ashely runs an ice-white polished fingernail over one of the four carved-wood bedposts. "And gorgeous. Nikolaos has incredible taste in antiques. The pieces he finds are timeless."

"They are. The last man I lived with had me there just to decorate for him. Most bachelors are hopeless, but this place is gorgeous."

"Nikolaos makes excellent choices." I hear a note of admiration in her voice when she speaks of him. She's a cute girl. Curvy and eager. I wonder if there's anything going on there...

"Let me lay your day out for you," she says. "We have an amazing deep tub in this bathroom. Don't know if you've seen it yet, but once you're ready for your day, let me know and we'll fetch Dr. Williams from the mainland."

"Ah. The doctor. Okay. Thank you." He mentioned a mandatory checkup, but I had no idea he'd schedule it so soon.

Maybe he wants to be rid of me...

"Take your time, make yourself at home—well, not exactly." She gives an easy laugh. "We don't want you lifting a finger, so let us do all the work, but other than that, make yourself at home, please. Let us know if you need anything."

"Okay, will do." At home, I'm the one running around, helping, planning, making others' ideas come to fruition. I'm not sure what I'll do with myself here.

"Oh, and whatever you do, don't go to the boathouse." Her bright gaze darkens. "Please? Thanks."

Her shiny blonde hair cascades like a waterfall down her back as she turns to leave. Before I can answer her, she's gone.

What is it with this boathouse?

Honestly? At this point? It's almost as if they're goading me to go into the boathouse. It's annoying. The more they tell me to stay away, the more I want to check it out. I have a nosy little streak in me, don't I? My hot pink she-devil whispers in my ear, *Nosy? Is that a bad thing? Last time you got nosy, you had the time of your life!*

She's right... Heat rises between my thighs at the memory of the alleyway. Then I remember what happened afterward. The sadness. The disappointment.

Maybe I will mind my own business this time.

I take my time showering in the oversized shower. Several jets of warm water stream out from showerheads planted in the stone wall, massaging my body. I lather my hair twice, slathering it in a lavender deep conditioner I found on the stocked shelves. I comb through the tangles from the boat ride.

Thinking of the upcoming intrusive doctor's visit, I shave everywhere. After, as I massage lotion into my smooth skin, I can't help but think of Nikolaos's hands on my body. There's no way I'm going down that road on this trip. I will not be getting naked in front of him. Just the doctor. That's the only reason I'm taking so much care with my preparations.

Right?

My little she-devil says, *more like yeah, right.*

I blow-dry my hair until it falls smooth over my shoulders. A touch of makeup and I'm good to go. I stick with the comfy clothing, opting for black leggings and a white long-sleeved cropped tee.

I wander down the spiral staircase, taking in the ornate carvings, feeling the smooth wood under my hand as I make my way down to the foyer. I need to find Ashely, to let her know I'm ready for the doctor. Nervous butterflies brush against the insides of my belly, wondering what Dr. Williams will find.

I look left, toward the library, then right, where the main living room is. As I'm deciding which way to go to look for Ashely, a staff member pops up, practically appearing out of the woodwork.

A young woman with purple streaks running through her short ponytail pushes the purple plastic frames of her glasses up the bridge of her nose as she greets me. "Hello, Ms. Charlie. Can I help you?"

I think back to my introductions last night, trying to remember her name. *Glasses for Gracies.* "Ah, yes, Gracie. I was looking for Ashely, to tell her I'm ready for... I'm ready."

"Of course!" Gracie chirps. "I'll tell her right away. Can I get you anything in the meantime? A mimosa? Another coffee?" Her glasses slide down and she pops them back up with a chipped black fingernail. I remember "scattered but brilliant" as the words used to describe her.

My stomach flips at the idea of drinking anything right now. "No, thank you. I'm just fine."

She eyes me for a moment, sizing me up like she can sense what I might like. "Well, what would you like to do while you wait? Something quiet? Reading? Mr. Bachman has an exceptionally well-stocked library. I could have someone start a fire for you in there if you'd like to read."

She nailed me. I'm impressed. He's done well in his hiring.

I think of the cushy brown leather chairs I spotted in the library during my tour of the castle last night. "That sounds nice, actually. But no need to trouble your team. I'll be happy with just a book."

Despite my protests, fifteen minutes later I'm seated in that cozy chair, my feet propped up on a worn leather ottoman, warming by a roaring fire. A thick blanket covers my lap. I've been told it's mine to keep—a guest takeaway gift. A colorful photo of the castle has been woven into one side, while the other side is a soft white sherpa fleece. I've got a hot chocolate with fresh whipped cream topped with curls of peppermint bark sitting on the table beside me and a leather-bound book in my hands. I bring the pages to my face, inhaling the soft scent of the delicate paper.

Books. Is there any better pleasure in this world? And to have access to such a gorgeous collection, each book bound in leather with gold gilding the pages, is almost heaven. I've missed Emilia's library at Liam's house. I don't think I've picked up a book since I returned to the Village. I'm so lost in my little world, I forget all about the upcoming appointment.

My stomach sinks when there's a light tap on the frame of the door.

Ashely's sweet voice draws me out of my story. "Charlie? Dr. Williams is ready for you now."

Remembering my page number, I carefully close the book and set it on the table beside the now empty mug. I go to clear it away, but Ashely stops me. "Oh, no, no. Please. Leave that. We'll get it later." She hurries around me, standing between me and the table, physically blocking me from picking up the cup.

She takes her job very seriously. "Um, where are we doing this?" I ask, glancing around the library.

She gives me a bright smile. "We have a full medical wing in the west end of the castle. Nikolaos and I have done everything we can to make it as comfortable as possible. I think you'll be pleased."

"You have a full medical room? Of course you do. Nikolaos is a Bachman, after all. And if Bachmans are anything, it's over-the-top."

"I know. And I absolutely adore it." She slips out of her professional demeanor for just a moment, the confession slipping from her lips. "What I wouldn't give to be a Beauty."

"It's wonderful," I say.

She flushes, looking as if she's feeling like she's crossed a line. "Let's go. Wouldn't want to keep Dr. Williams waiting." She flutters from the room, and I follow behind her.

Would she want Nikolaos to be the Bachman to make her a Beauty? I shove the thought away. Good for her if she does. I had my chance with him. I could have taken him up on any one of the offers he made in his phone calls to go out with him.

The medical wing looks like none I've ever seen. I'm taken to a sunny room with a big window facing the lake, hung with fluttery curtains. There's another roaring fire in a deep stone fireplace. There's a brass-framed bed, the head of it lifted up in a reclining position. Several soft looking quilts lay neatly over the bed, their star patterns formed from brightly colored triangles. Tucked to the side is standard medical equipment, but in such a pleasant room they don't seem so sterile.

A friendly looking woman with copper ringlets and a bright smile waits for me on a wing-backed chair. She's wearing a floral dress.

Have to say, I love the pattern. It's different shades of pink roses, their petals threaded with gold.

I like her even more.

She stands, offering me her hand. "Hello, Charlie! Lovely to meet you. I'm Dr. Williams, but you can call me Tanesha if that makes you feel more comfortable. I'd like to start with us just sitting in front of the fire chatting if that's alright with you. I prefer an old school, midwife approach to gynecology. A more comfy, natural approach, while still keeping up with all the cutting-edge research in my field. But if you'd feel better with me wearing a white lab coat and calling me doctor, we can shift to a more clinical feel."

"No. Please. This is just perfect. Comfy and cozy. I love it." I take a seat in the empty chair across from her. "Thank you for coming all this way. I'm sorry you had to travel for me."

She shakes her head, waving her hands in front of her, dismissing my apologies. "Please. I'm thrilled to be here. Nikolaos is a personal friend of mine and after hearing what you've gone through, I'm very happy to be here for you. Can you tell me a little more about yourself?"

We go through some pleasant small talk that eases into my medical history. Then we get to the hard part, but I find talking to another woman about what happened a relief, not a burden. When I finish telling her my story, I feel lighter somehow.

She speaks gently and slowly. "I'm going to run some blood tests, check you out, but honestly, the issue you had is usually a one-time-only thing. I know the experience was absolutely devastating, but I want you to know it's highly unlikely that the same thing would happen to you a second time."

The breath I've been holding since she started talking releases slowly from my lungs. "Really?"

"Really, really." She gives my hand a reassuring pat. "If you'd like, we can dive deeper, do some genetic testing as well to put your mind at ease if you'd like to try and conceive again."

Try and conceive? I shake my head. "We weren't... trying."

Her voice is soft as she places a gentle hand over mine. "Would you like to have a baby one day?"

More than anything in this world, Dr. Williams. My hand goes to my belly, thinking of the warm, happy, magical feeling that came over me when that little plus sign popped up. "One day, I would like to."

"Then let's do all the tests. Why not?" After the exam, she assures me everything looks healthy, and she'll get back to me with the results of the testing as soon as she can.

Now that the appointment is over, what happens next? Does Nikolaos take me back to the mainland or do I go on my own? The thought of walking into my dark house alone makes my stomach drop.

It's just so warm here with the fireplaces. And the cocoa. And the books.

Would anyone miss me if I just snuck back into the library?

I'm padding down the hall, sneaking back to the library, when the sound of a scream grabs my attention. I run to the nearest window to see if I hear it again. A moment later, I do. High pitched and filled with fear, it's definitely the scream of a woman. The sound runs through me, sending shivers down my spine. Hearing it for the second time, I can't deny what I've heard.

It sounds like it's coming from near the lake.

From the boathouse.

CHAPTER TEN

Beast

She slips up to her room, I can only assume to grab her sneakers. There's no way she's not planning on running toward that scream. Anyone on this island would have heard it. Are my gut instincts on point? They usually seem to be with this woman. I wait behind the curve of the staircase to catch the naughty girl in action.

Ready to pounce.

One minute later, Nancy Drew appears. Her hair has been pulled back in a high ponytail, giving her a girlish look, and she now has on sneakers. Her gumshoes, I suppose. She peers down from the upstairs landing, assumes the coast is clear, and tiptoes her way down the stairs. To her investigative credit, she doesn't make a sound in her descent.

Just as the sole of her shoe hits the final tread I step out from the shadows.

And there it is.

That look on her face I've been standing here waiting to see. Emotions erupt in her gaze, caught somewhere between startled and terrified. A flush rises, warming the pretty apples of her cheeks. She knows she's naughty and she's been caught.

Her reaction makes my cock throb hard in my jeans, her surprised look reminding me of her face that night in the alleyway when I caught her nosing around where she didn't belong, and then the intense pleasure of having my cock between those lush lips.

"What are you up to, pretty girl?" I wrap my hand around the curve of the banister, moving to the foot of the stairs, blocking her way.

She glances down at me, dark lashes fluttering. "I... um... I— thought I heard a scream."

"And you thought you'd investigate?" My gaze lowers to the curve of her breasts, her nipples straining against the fabric of her thin white top. The shirt is cropped, and my gaze lowers further to an enticing slice of her bare belly that peeks out from above the waistband of her black leggings. "Tell me. Where were you headed, Nancy Drew?"

"I'm more of a Fancy Nancy than a Nancy Drew." She twirls the end of her ponytail around her manicured fingernails, pearly white teeth sinking into her bottom lip.

"Changing the subject on me, huh, Fancy Nancy?" I throw a heavy boot onto the bottom step, my denim-clad thigh stretched out perfectly in a way that makes me want to throw her over the top of it, spank the fullest part of her ass, and make it jiggle.

She jumps as the sole of my boot hits the stairstep. "*Nooo...* I'm just choosing to evade the question."

"I don't like that. I like direct answers." I can't stop my fingers from reaching out, stroking that smooth band of skin of her exposed belly.

She trembles under my touch, the flush in her cheeks blooming to a rosy red. "Well, if you want a direct answer, then tell me you can handle one."

I have to chuckle at that. "Look at me. You think there's something you could throw at me, little girl, that I couldn't handle?"

Glancing down she gives my thigh a wary look, her brows knitting together. "I mean, handle it without getting ticked off and tossing me over that thigh of yours."

I stroke the top of my thigh with a splayed-out palm. The simple gesture makes her nipples tighten further, making my cock throb even more. "Now why would your answer to my question make me want to toss you over my thigh? I can only think of one thing that would make me want to punish that gorgeous ass of yours right now, and that would be if you were headed to the one place I specifically asked you not to go."

The color drains from her face.

I reach up, brushing the pad of my thumb over those gorgeous lips of hers. "Tell me. Where were you going?"

To her credit, she meets my eyes, holding my gaze as she answers me. "The boathouse."

"I like your honesty."

She nods. "Thank you."

"But I don't like your answer. It makes me angry."

A shimmer of fear flashes over her features. She takes a deep breath, gulping down her nerves, and tosses her hands on her hips.

"Yes. I was headed to the boathouse. Like I told you, I heard a woman's scream, and I was going to investigate."

"How do you know you heard a woman scream and not a fox or something?"

Her brow narrows at me. "I know what I heard."

"Regardless of what you heard, tell me what I told you last night when I brought you here."

She looks away, protesting. "Not to go to the boathouse, but that doesn't matter when I heard what I heard—"

I capture her chin in my hand, stopping her words. "What I say is the only thing that matters on this island. My word is law. And you were about to break the law."

"About to." She holds up a manicured finger. "But didn't. Could have, but didn't."

"Only because I stopped you." I glance down at the plane of my chest. I'm literally a wall keeping her from going about her snooping. I need to do something to ensure this little escapade is her last. Obviously, she needs more than a warning to keep her where she's supposed to be.

Our bodies are so close, I can feel the heat coming off her, hear her quickened intake of breath. Smell the lavender scent of her hair. My cock demands her. I can't keep my hands off her another second. I have to have her.

And why shouldn't I? She's basically mine, trapped on my island, her body responding so sensually to the proximity of mine. I told myself I'd keep my hands off her, focus on my work. Get her checked out and send her on her way.

The doctor has cleared her.

There's no real reason for her to be here.

But now, with our gazes locked and the tension between us so palpable you could reach out and snap it, I know I was fooling myself all along.

She's not going anywhere.

I'm not letting her.

She senses me ready to make my move, a predator stalking its prey, ready to pounce. There's a flash of decision-making in her hazel eyes. She does what I know she's going to do. Tries to make a break for it. There's no way past me so she turns on her sneakered heel, hoping to dash up the stairs.

It's too easy. I don't even have to move off the stair where I stand, reaching out, my hands locking around her waist. She gives a pretty little shriek as I tip her over my thigh, pinning her right where I imagined, wrapping my right arm around her waist, locking her tight against me. The curves of her ass are propped up on my thigh, her dangling legs finding purchase on a stair. Her ponytail falls forward, brushing the edge of the stairs, and her hands press into the soft carpet runner.

This is going to be fun.

"Is this really necessary?" she hisses. "With your staff all around?"

"There's no one here. Besides, my staff, unlike you, know to mind their own business." I bring my palm down on the center of her ass with a hard spank. "But you'll learn. I'll teach you."

She wriggles her hips, sucking air between her teeth in pain. "Oooh! You are unbelievable. You know that?"

God, that wiggling. Her hip digs into my cock, making me hard. I know she feels my hardening erection pressing against her. She gives a little gasp, feeling its size. She knows what it's capable of making her feel.

I give a growl. "You're acting all upset but I bet if I slipped my fingers down your panties right now, your pretty pussy would be all wet for me."

My filthy accusation makes her gasp again. She snaps back, "Is that all you think about? Sex?"

"No. Only when I'm with you." Which is a lie. I think about having sex with her all the time. When I'm working. When I'm alone. When I'm stroking my cock in the shower in the morning. Yes. All I think about is her pretty smile, her beautiful body, fucking that perfect pussy of hers.

I've been with plenty of beautiful, sexy women.

There's just something about Charlie that sets her apart, makes me put work second, made me steal her away to my castle. She's got this undeniable sexy side to her, but I could also see her being the mother of my child, welcoming me home with a hot, home-cooked meal.

What the actual fuck? *Get back to what you're best at, Beast. Getting what you need and moving on.* I slip my hand down the back of her stretchy leggings, expecting to feel panties. My hand is met with warm flesh.

I can't stop the groan that rises in my chest. "No panties. Again? Are you trying to kill me?" My cock jolts against her.

"Looks better without when you're wearing leggings," she snaps matter-of-factly.

"Lucky me, that you're so fashion conscious." My fingers find their way over her ass, sneaking between the tops of her thighs, fingering her from behind. Holy shit, she's even wetter than I thought she'd be. My fingers are slick and I push them further, circling her clit.

She moans, her hips moving against me in earnest now. That roll of her hips, it's my undoing. I tear her leggings down, pull my thigh out from under her and push her onto her hands and knees on the stairs.

I rip my belt buckle open and free my aching cock. Kneeling down, I slam into her. "God, you're so tight, so wet. You're gonna make me come, babygirl."

"Not before me." Her raspy words surprise me, turning me on even more.

I slap what I can reach of her bare ass. "You'll come when I tell you to." I reach around her waist, finding her clit. I finger it as I thrust into her.

Her pussy locks tight around me, milking my cock. She's so close and so am I but I won't let her come till she asks for it.

I pinch her clit between my forefinger and thumb, keeping my cock buried in her and I hold like that, leaving her panting with frustration. "You want to come, pretty girl?"

"Yes. God, yes! Let me come already."

"Beg for it."

Her face tips over her shoulder, a look of desperation shooting from her glazed-over eyes. "Are you serious?"

I move, just a tiny bit, pulling my cock back then thrusting it into her, still holding her clit. "What do you think."

"You, sir, are infuriating. Please, Nikolaos. Let me come!"

It's the first time I've heard my name on her pretty pink lips. It makes my balls tighten, the cum ready for the climax growing in my core. I can't hold back any longer, she just turns me on so fucking much. Everything she does, every sexy little breath she pants out. I rub her clit, moving my hips, gyrating against her as I fuck her, hard and fast, bringing her to her peak of pleasure.

She locks down on me like a vise, her hand reaching behind her, grabbing at me, tugging on my shirt. "Oh my God. Nikolaos!"

She says my name again and I fucking lose it. I grab her hips, holding her as close to me as I can, buried as deeply inside of her as I can be. My cock gives a hard twitch, cum shooting from me, filling her pussy with my seed.

I lean down, moving her hair from her face, my mouth finding hers. I lean over her, kissing her, my tongue claiming her mouth as my body has just claimed hers. Something passes between us in that kiss, that strange burning returning to my chest, my empty core aching as if my desires haven't just been fulfilled.

I pull away so I can look at her. Her eyes turn up to meet mine, that invisible energy that binds us holding our gazes together. Neither of us mentions the fact we didn't use a condom.

Again.

Let the chips fall where they may.

CHAPTER ELEVEN

Charlie

I can't believe I let him do this again. Not that he seemed like he'd be taking no for an answer, but to have unprotected sex with him again? What on earth is wrong with me? Is my self-respect so low that I would let him use me like this?

Or do I just want a baby so darn bad I'm willing to risk anything to get there. My only comfort? I haven't gotten my period since... the incident. So I'm safe. Right?

Gawd. What was I thinking?

The truth? The cold hard truth? I wasn't thinking at all. My brain, my mind, had nothing to do with what happened. It was all my body's doing. My body and that darn little pink she-devil on my shoulder, begging me to beg him to make me come. I was so wet, dripping wet for him, when he dipped his fingers inside me, I almost burst right then and there.

His touch, his body, heck, that woodsy scent that he carries with him. I can't resist him. But he's a dangerous man. One I shouldn't be involved with. And there's the small matter of the scream I heard and whatever is going on at the boathouse.

Regardless of the mistake I just made, I still want to know what is going on here on Dark Island. I could leave; I'm sure he would let me if I asked. Or I could stay.

I'm going to investigate. Once I put my mind at ease that there's nothing to report back to the family, I'll leave. And if I leave with a baby in my belly, so be it. I know what I just did was reckless and irresponsible, but it's done.

I'll wait till it's dark outside. Then, I'll sneak out, go to the boathouse, and see what I can find. I take a quick shower, scrubbing him from between my thighs. I dress in clean, comfy clothes. What time is it? It's not even noon. What to do with my day?

As if reading my mind, Gracie comes floating by the open bedroom door, peeking her head into the room. She adjusts her glasses' frames. "Miss Charlie! Is there anything I can do for you?"

I think of those creamy chocolate crepes I had for breakfast. The Beauties would love those at our next Beauties Brunch. "May I speak with the chef? If he's not too busy?"

"Of course! Follow me." She leads me down to the big commercial kitchen in the back wing of the castle. Chef Remy is standing behind an enormous stainless steel island, rolling out dough.

I make a few minutes of small talk with Remy, working up the courage to ask a favor. "I'd love to see if there's a way to have some of your crepes shipped to the city for an event I'm having. They were so delicious, and I know my friends would love them."

"No." He shakes his head, almost as if he's angry with me.

I'm not used to being refused by the staff here. "No?"

"No. Crepes cannot be shipped. That would be a sin." I see. He's not angry. Just passionate. "They must be made fresh and served immediately. Come. I'll show you."

"You'll show me how to make them?"

"Yes. Of course. Come." He goes to the wall, pulling a black apron that matches the one he wears down from a hook. He hands me the apron. "Mr. Bachman is very fond of the boysenberry ones."

There's no way in this world I'll ever be cooking for the Beast. I pull on the apron, tying the strings together.

"Is he?" I ask, being polite.

"He is. I was surprised when he hired me over a Greek chef, thinking he'd want meals from his homeland, but no, the man has excellent taste in food. He went with France." He flashes me a grin.

"He chose well. That's for sure." I love how much pride this man takes in his work. And, so far, I love his food.

He gets right to work, showing me how to whisk the thin batter. I follow his orders and soon we have a plate of boysenberry crepes. He lets me use the sifter to snow powdered sugar over their tops.

"Perfect," he says, taking the plate from me. "I'll send these to the master of the house, compliments of you, Miss Charlie."

"Oh!" Is that a good idea? Sending food to Nikolaos would give him the wrong impression of my intentions. Especially after what we did this morning. "Oh! I don't know—" But Remy's already handing the plate to his assistant, sending him on his way.

Ashely comes in, looping her arm in mine, rushing me from the kitchen. "Miss Charlie. We thought you'd like to see the gardens and the greenhouse. Mr. Bachman told us you're fond of flowers."

"I am. That would be wonderful. Thanks." She tours me around the lush gardens filled with lots of evergreen plants, but many things are dormant this time of the year so I have to use my imagination to fill in the fruits and vegetables that will be budding here in the spring.

"So as you saw, the garden is mostly hibernating for the winter, which is why we have this." We step out from behind the brick wall of the garden to find a greenhouse, almost as big as the boathouse. We step inside and the air is warm and wet, humid like a summer day. Ashely closes the door, shutting out the cold. "What do you think?"

"It's amazing." I walk slowly down the rows of tables where beautiful flowers are growing in their pots. Geraniums, their little floral bunches not only in red and white but apricot and yellow as well. Gazania treasure flowers in vivid shades of orange and pink. Burnt orange and bright yellow chrysanthemums. I spot the popcorn flowers growing on the left-hand side of the greenhouse, the ones that fill the foyer. Then there're more exotic blooms as well, orchids and hibiscus, and Chef Remy has his own herb garden with lemon verbena, pineapple sage and sweet basil, each of their names clearly labeled on black stickers. "It's like springtime in the dead of winter."

"Isn't it just magical?" She glances at her watch, then back up at me. "And now we have to get you back to your rooms for a light lunch as well as dinner preparations."

"Dinner preparations? Will I be cooking again?"

She gives a little laugh. "Absolutely not. Chef was happy to show you how to make crepes, but dinner? That's his domain and no one other than his assistant is allowed in the kitchen when he's cooking his courses. Not even me. Besides, Nikolaos would have our heads if we put you to work."

That little flush creeps back in her cheeks at the mention of her boss. I don't think I'm imagining it… there're feelings there, I'm sure of it. How deep they run, only Ashely knows.

Back at my rooms, I find a spread enough for five women. Champagne nestles in a silver bucket, buried in ice. Little sandwiches line a three-tiered tray, their crusts cut off. Fresh fruit sits in bowls and slivers of beef and different cheeses have been laid out beautifully on plates.

I look at Ashely. "All this for me?"

"Yes. Have all you want but don't worry. Whatever you don't eat the girls—" Her face goes blank, and she quickly corrects herself, "the *staff* will snack on later. Mr. Bachman feels very strongly about not wasting food. Something to do with his life before all this…"

She doesn't elaborate further. I wonder if he faced the same neglect I did as a child. I also want to know why she said "girls" originally instead of staff, because I know his team is coed. Something fishy is going down on this island. It's like they're purposely keeping me busy…

Are they?

Taking me on all these little tours and errands, keeping me away from the one place I need to go.

The boathouse.

Call me shallow but my detective work is put on the backburner when they bring in the gowns. It takes three staff members to roll in the cart that holds all of the dresses. Gorgeous, bright flowery patterns burst from the fabrics. I flip through the gowns, smiling at each one.

There's one little sleek black dress hiding in the middle of all the colorful dresses. The neckline plunges low, the back even lower.

There's a slit up the side of the gown. The dress is basically sex on a hanger.

I can't help but imagine his face when he sees me in this. My fingers glide over the silky fabric. "This one. This is the one. Please."

Ashely gives a little smirk. "That's the one he requested."

"What do you mean?"

"He told the shop to send mostly floral prints, that that's what you prefer, but to throw in one sexy little black dress." What looks like a little wave of jealousy passes over her face. "Just in case."

I'm curious. What exactly did he say about me? I ask, "In case what?"

Her face goes bright pink. "He just said he'd like to see you in black. He thinks it would…" She actually has to stop and clear her throat to continue. Her gaze breaks away from mine to the dress. "Bring out your naughty side."

"Oh, did he?"

I try to will the heat that's forming between my thighs to melt away. He's the thing that brings out my naughty side, not a dress. Every time I'm around him I seem to do something more reckless than the last.

Ashely helps me dress. I'm a little shy, having to strip completely down before putting on the dress, but there is no wearing a bra with it. And panties I really don't bother with anyway.

I must have imagined the jealous moment because as soon as I slip into the gown, she's fluttering around me, showering me with compliments. "You look amazing! Like this dress was made for you."

I smooth my hand over my sleek, freshly flat-ironed hair, looking in the antique floor-length mirror that sits in the corner of the room. Pink flowers and curls gone, my usual string of pearls missing from my neck, I don't look like myself at all.

Charlie 2.0. The sex goddess.

Ashely politely dismisses herself to let me finish getting ready. I turn, glancing over my shoulder, in awe of the low line of the back, dipping to just above the curve of my ass. I lift the dress, shifting the slit over my bare leg to admire the strappy rhinestone sandals Ashely brought me. I painted my finger and toenails a sexy shade of red I'd normally steer away from, always opting for a pale, neutral pink.

There's a knock. The door opens before I can answer. As good as I think I might look, all thoughts of my own appearance dissipate into the night the moment he walks into my room.

I'm not one to curse, but...

Gosh. Darn.

He looks so incredible if I was wearing panties they'd have melted off. Nikolaos wears a black suit, perfectly tailored to fit his large frame. A light gray shirt underneath, the top button left undone. His thick hair is gelled back, his face freshly shaven. The light woodsy scent of his cologne reaches me.

Good grief, the man looks so gorgeous I can't help but wonder what our baby would have looked like... Little pink she-devil says, *Girl, keep doing the nasty with that Greek god and you're gonna find out.*

Charlie! Get a hold of yourself.

He takes me in from the top of my head to the stiletto sandals on my feet. "God. Damn. You look incredible."

"Was just thinking the same thing about you. Although more of a PG-13 version."

I suddenly feel shy, wondering if this whole sexy façade is really me.

His gaze heats further. "I've got plans for you. Come." A heavy silver watch flashes on his wrist as he beckons to me.

Nervous butterfly wings tickle my belly. I take the arm he offers me. "Where are we going?"

"A place you seem interested in touring." He gives me a hard stare.

The boathouse! Finally I'll get to put this mystery to bed without sneaking around under the cover of night.

I keep my voice calm and even. "Oh yeah? Where to?"

"My dungeon." The lust-filled smile he gives me heats my core.

Oh my gosh. His dungeon. His sex rooms! My stomach flip-flops, a white-hot heat trickling over my body. What kinds of torturous devices does he have down there? And will he ask for my consent before he uses them on me, or will he just do what he wants, regardless of my possible protests?

I tell my body not to break out in a sweat and risk ruining the delicate fabric of my dress. My sex clenches with each step I take, anticipating what's to come. As we descend the stairs, I realize how crazy this is. That I'm still here. That I allowed him to have unprotected sex with me on his stairs, and now to lure me down to his seedy dungeon...

Right off the foyer there's a small black door I missed before, its top shaped in an arch. The handle is a black iron ring. He pulls on it, the door opening to reveal a narrow stone staircase that curves as it lowers to the basement of the four-story tower.

"Careful." He holds my arm tight, protecting me from stumbling in my heels.

"Thank you." I cling to him, deciding it's best to lean on him as I navigate this narrow passage. We reach the bottom safely and the space opens up. The stone floor has been lacquered and polished and it shines under the flickering lights of the chandelier that hangs above our heads.

He moves forward, to another black, arched door.

Here we go. Clips of films from the Fifty Shades franchise flicker through my brain as he reaches for the handle. Whips and chains and leather belts dance through my mind. As I suck in a deep breath, the white heat of fear takes me over. My knees go to jelly, and I tear my hand away from his.

"I can't do this!" The words burst forth from me as I take a shaky step backward. "I can't go in there with you."

"Why not?" He's so loving this, getting off on my fear. His hand slides into the pocket of his suit pants, probably adjusting his stiffening cock. He does so love to scare me.

"I can't go in your dirty sex dungeon, I'm just not that kind of girl. I'm sorry, but I'm not. I love this dress, I love the way I look tonight, but I'm *Charlie*. Flowers and pearls, and the most dangerous thing I do in a day is overeat chocolate."

"What about wine?" he asks.

"Huh? What do you mean?" I wrap an arm around my belly, my other hand tugging on a strand of hair as I twirl it around a finger. "Of course I like wine."

"Then I think you're going to love my dungeon." He pushes the door open. "Welcome to my speakeasy."

"What?" I follow behind him into a room that's been converted into a sexy little bar, the design so sultry and beautiful I just stare. Black leather walls, a mirrored ceiling, more gold chandeliers, light flickering from their modern lines. A polished dark wood bar stretches across one side of the room, complete with a bartender, a young man dressed in black standing at attention waiting to take our order.

High-top two-seater bistro tables dot the room, a single red rose in a black vase sitting in the center of each tabletop. He leads me to one that has small bites laid out on plates. Savory puffed pastries alongside what look like chouquettes, French pastry sugar puffs.

I feel so silly, assuming he wanted to do naughty things with me. What happened on the stairs earlier was just a punishment that got carried away. He's only inviting me for a drink. Is that a dip of disappointment tugging at my belly?

He holds out a chair for me. Such a gentlemen right now, after teasing me so ruthlessly. I slip into the cool leather seat. "Thank you."

He takes the seat across from me. "What would you like to drink? Red? White? Champagne?"

The idea of champagne reminds me of that first night I grabbed a second flute from the passing tray and how it lowered my inhibitions, leading me to the alleyway. After our crazy rendezvous on the stairs this morning, I think I'll play it safe. "Red, please."

I nibble at a chouquette as he goes to the bar to get our drinks. It's better than any I've had in France. Remy strikes again. Beast returns with two generous pours of red wine.

We sip at the wine. Like the champagne in my room earlier, it's delicious. He's got good taste. It's a comfortable silence but could soon grow awkward. Do I start the small talk? Do I wait for him to speak?

"There's a hidden tunnel just off of this room. It leads to another boathouse. One you're actually allowed in." He gives a lusty grin like he's thinking of my earlier spanking.

A secret tunnel? This could be good. Could be helpful for tonight. I keep the curious Nancy Drew tone out of my voice. "Oh, really. And what's in that boathouse?"

"A boat. But what's incredible is that there's a waterway running through the boathouse. It leads right to the lake. Back in Prohibition it was used to smuggle in liquor. And this was an actual underground bar. People would travel out here from the city to party. I tried to bring back some of the history of the castle as I renovated it."

I'm intrigued. I ask him more questions about his renovation, the castle, and the history of the property. I'm surprised to find how easy he is to talk to when he's in his own space, relaxed like this, a glass of rich wine in his hand. There's no break in our conversation; it flows like we've known one another forever.

Even though I really know nothing about him.

I'm having such a nice time I almost forget the mission I have to put in motion tonight. My stomach flip-flops, wondering if this time I'll be able to pull it off. As he takes my hand to lead me to the boat, my nervous energy keys up, knowing what I have to do later tonight.

As we walk through the hidden tunnel, I almost think I hear the faint sound of a scream.

CHAPTER TWELVE

Beast

The boat waits for us on the waterway. It's a narrow riverboat that I've had brought back to life, its cabins filled with honey-colored wood. The channel of aqua water is lit with white lights from beneath, and the smooth surface of the water sparkles under the soft glow of additional lights overhead. The table is already set, a white cloth covering it, tall white candles flickering against the smooth, lacquered walls. The boat remains stationary, bobbing in the waterway here in the boathouse, a little floating restaurant.

We drink more wine and dine on filet mignon, roasted baby potatoes, and vegetables sautéed in one of Remy's herb butter sauces. The conversation is light. She asks about the castle's renovations, a subject I find myself able to easily discuss for hours.

The moment I stepped foot on this property, I knew it was mine. The day I closed and got the keys to the castle, I felt settled, like the last piece of my life had fallen into place. I'd been training to be a

Bachman for a year. I was finally a brother, and now I had a place of my own.

One that would be perfect to help us take on our next top secret family project.

Dinner moves too quickly, her company so easy, I'm surprised to find I've already cleaned my plate.

With the tines of my fork, I point at the last piece of steak on her plate. "Do you want the rest of that?"

"No, thank you. I'm finished." She pushes the plate toward me. "Go for it."

She gives me that look that lets me know she's about to pry. "Ashely said you have a thing about not wasting food. Any particular reason?"

"Yeah. Not having it when I was a kid." I pop the steak into my mouth. Tender. Flavorful. I would have killed for a meal like this when I was growing up.

"I only eat until I'm full, not having the grace of you guys' metabolism, but I do know what it means to go without." Her voice goes to a whisper, her focus on the corner of the cloth napkin she unfolds and re-folds on her lap. "I know the feeling."

I'm intrigued. How can such a put-together woman have come from desperate circumstances? Scratch that. My background is the reason for my success. It's probably the same for her.

I want to know more. "Tell me yours and I'll tell you mine."

She shrugs. "You know the story. Single mom, working long hours, couldn't afford childcare. Couldn't or wouldn't, I'm not so sure anymore. The majority of my mother's budget went to the bars she frequented most nights. My earliest memories are of me being home alone. Making PB&J for dinner, or peanut butter crackers. I wasn't allowed to use the oven or the microwave. She seemed fine with it, but she must have felt guilty because every so often, she'd leave a bar of milk chocolate on the table."

"First memories?" I feel my brow crease. "How young?"

"Five? Maybe six?"

Holy shit. I try to picture little Charlie, standing on a stool, trying to reach the kitchen counter to make her own meal. "Is that even legal?"

"Don't think so." She gives a sad little laugh. "Mom liked to go out at night. I got myself ready for school. Rode the bus. Teachers would question me when I never showed up to school events and my mom didn't come to the parent-teacher conferences, but overall, I was a tough little kid, and I took care of myself. So, no one noticed how alone I really was."

"Unbelievable." I want to tear her mother to pieces. Who neglects someone as special as Charlie? "Have you forgiven her?"

She nods. "Yes. But I don't speak to her. Haven't wanted to for years. Not since I met my real family."

"Same. Thank the gods for the Bachmans." My throat goes all tight and I take a sip of my wine.

Thank the gods? I don't say stuff like that… Why am I opening up? I've never discussed my past with anyone. Why her?

But the words still come. "My single mother had priorities other than mothering as well. Mainly drunk men with heavy fists. I left as soon as I realized I couldn't save her. But when I was young, there were a lot of nights with little to no food on the table." I take a deep sip of my drink. "It was only when I grew up that I realized it's not that hard to put food on the table, not if you really want to."

Her eyes snap up to meet mine. "I've had the exact same thought. Word for word. If I had a child, they'd want for nothing…"

Her words trail off, her thoughts most likely going to our pregnancy.

I grab her hand in mine on the tabletop. "Same. Sure, my ways of making money are a little questionable, but I could have provided, would have provided, if I needed to. I would have made it work."

"Now look at us." She smiles but her eyes are sad. "Neither of us wants for anything."

Unspoken truth hangs between us. She wants a baby. I want her. And maybe… I want… a baby, too. Ever since I first heard she was pregnant, I've had this nagging little visual of me and Charlie, baby making three, in the back of my mind.

It's slowly making its way to the forefront.

I lift my glass. "To the Bachmans."

She lifts her glass, tipping it to clink with mine. "To the Bachmans."

She takes a long sip of her wine, looking off in the distance as she speaks. "I think that's what really drew me to the family in the first place. Chosen family. And a gaggle of Beauties. I knew I would never be alone again. Then I lost a fiancé and, on my honeymoon, a husband. But still, I'm not alone. I have the family."

"Chosen family. I like that."

"After my first fiancé died, I needed a change. I started going by my middle name, Charlie. And I dyed my hair from blonde to brown, no longer wanting to be that lonely little girl." She sighs, the rest of the words rushing out of her. "Then my husband died, and I decided I was cursed and gave up on love altogether."

I'd heard about her crazy past, but I certainly don't believe she's cursed. Some of us just aren't meant for love. I tip my drink back, finishing it off.

"Work is my one true love," I say. "I'd do anything for this family."

There's a glint of determination in her gaze, her eyes leveling with mine. "So would I." She tips her glass back, finishing her own drink.

I can't tear my eyes off her lips, now red from her wine. I want more. Our sex on the stairs left me somewhat satiated but my desire for her still simmers under the surface, threatening to boil over. I know I could have her right this second, just pull out her chair, bend her over it and take her.

But she looks too pretty to be treated like that. And that thought disturbs me. It's like I have too much respect for her, I care for her needs too often.

Think of her often.

I think of her too much.

Do I keep her here? What am I even doing, having dinner with her like this? I don't treat women like this, showing them the private side of my life, letting them stay in my house, giving them full access to my staff.

She's different, and for the life of me I can't put my finger on why, other than she's just... her.

She's strong. Determined. I admire her guts to ask questions, to look for the truth. She just better keep her ass away from the boathouse like she's supposed to. She's just Charlie Bachman.

God, I've got to get my head out of the clouds and focus on work. I've got to cut this date—fuck, did I just call it that—short and get back to work. I've got a shipment coming in tonight. The largest one we've had to date. All the more reason to get her out of here, to send her back home.

Tomorrow. I'll do it tomorrow. Aiden can take her back to the mainland on the boat.

Now she's running the tip of her tongue over those red lips, begging me to steal a taste. Well, what the hell. Why not take her one more time before I put her on that boat to cross the lake back to the city.

Time to show her the place that hides behind my speakeasy.

My sex dungeon.

"I have one more place to show you." I take her hand. "Come."

She shoots me a look mixed with fear and trust as she rises from her chair with the grace of a ballerina. "I thought I'd had the whole tour."

"Almost." I think of my toys, trying to choose what tantalizing way I want to torture her. Breath play, wax play, tie her gorgeous body up in silk roping? What about a collar, pretty kitty cat ears and a butt plug tail...

Again, she looks so beautiful I don't even want to take off that dress. I just want to pull her down on my lap and have her ride me. I check my watch. I'm pressed for time. I'll take her down to the dungeon and show her my collection, letting that be the foreplay. I know that naughty streak in her is going to get her wet, just thinking of the things we could do.

It's not a dungeon, really, but a modern room with sleek lines, white plaster smoothed over the stone walls. My paddles and whips and leather straps are all black. They hang on the wall nice and neat, a beautiful display. A chain hangs down in the center of the room from the ceiling, leather cuffs dangling from it. I'd love to strap her wrists in while I have her fuck me but again... time.

I have to be on the shore in an hour. I can't be late.

"It's prettier than I thought it would be." She takes a turn around the room, looking at all the implements. She glances over her shoulder at me. "Sexy."

"I thought you'd like it down here. We don't have much time. I wanted to show you around, and then I thought," I cross the room, grabbing her up in my arms, "you could fuck me."

Her face flushes a pretty pink. She winds her arms around my neck. "Oh, you did, did you?"

"I did." I lean down, brushing a light kiss over her lips. I want to kiss her deeper, longer, but in the back of my mind, the clock is running, tick, tick, tick of the countdown. I drag an armless black leather chair to the center of the room. "We only have a few minutes. I want you quick and dirty. Just climb on my lap and fuck me."

I dip my hand under that high slit of her dress, raising it higher till I reach her pussy. No panties. Again. I groan, dipping my fingers in her wetness. My other hand goes to her breast, slipping under the low neckline. God. No bra either. This woman will be the death of me.

I squeeze her breast, her nipple tightening at my touch. I slip my hands from her. She gives a soft sigh as I sit down on the chair, pulling her onto my lap.

She leans down, kissing me as I work to hitch up her dress, gathering the material around her waist. Her legs spread, and she plants each high heel on the concrete floor on either side of my legs. I free my cock, this time slipping on a condom from my pocket. I grabbed it earlier. Just in case.

I grasp her hips, lifting her up. Her eyes lock on mine and we keep it that way as I enter her. I hold her hips tight, bringing her tight, wet pussy down onto my cock.

And I lose my mind.

A deep groan leaves me, and my mind goes blank. She runs her hands through my hair and the touch of her fingernails lightly running over the back of my head takes me to another level. My only thoughts are of how her sexy body feels wrapped around me and her light touch.

She knows what to do, obeying her body, rolling her hips and chasing her own pleasure. Her back arches and she leans her head back, exposing her beautiful neck. I take the opportunity to kiss, bite, and suck the delicate flesh there.

"You're so tight. You feel so fucking good. God, your pussy is perfection."

She gives a little giggle at my words. I dig my fingers into her hips, hoping to leave little circular bruises for her to find tomorrow. I lift my hips, bringing her down and burying myself further inside of her. Her head flies forward. She tucks her face into the curve of my shoulder.

"Oh my God. Oh my God," she pants.

She's getting close, her muscles tightening around me. And thank God because I can't hold back any longer. She feels too fucking good. She gives a little mewing cry, clutching me. I lift once more, giving one more good, hard thrust, and let go.

The climax is such an intense release, I can't think or breathe as it happens. It rips through me, cleansing my soul, warming my blood. When I come to, she's staring at me, a lazy look of pleasure on her face.

A face that I can't stop thinking about.

I ease her up off of me. "I wish I could stay with you, but I have some work I have to do tonight."

"Oh, yeah?" She gives me a curious look. "Anything to do with the boathouse?"

"I thought you gave up your investigating." I kiss her forehead, taking her by the hand to lead her to her room.

"I did. I was just curious."

"You remember what curious little girls get. Mind your business."

I leave her room, taking a moment to walk the grounds before I undertake the task ahead of me. I'd do anything for this family, take any risk. I still remember when Dante first started recruiting me for the Bachmans, wanting me to leave my post as an Air Marshal in the Greek military to join them.

He took me on a tour of the Parrish, the family's private island, wooing me like a bride. They'd started off with only a few boats purchased from the priests of a tiny Catholic chapel, hence the name Parrish. A hefty price was paid for the Bachman island to be documented as uninhabited. The island is home to the Mediterranean branch of the family that the American Bachmans love to visit.

The island is in the Aegean, the sea that separates Greece and Europe from Asia Minor. There's a second, smaller island for weapons storage. We even have our own landing strip for private jets.

Elegant, tasteful, three-story opulent homes made of white stone bless the island. Enormous glass windows overlook the turquoise sea. Marble floors, marble counters, verandas with ocean views on every level. Pristine wooden docks. Terracotta-colored patios dotted with black metal bistro tables. Each home is different, but they all sport red tile roofs and black shutters, and colorful flowers in wooden window boxes.

Children run freely, loved by parents, raised by all. Men are devoted to their women, and the rules for marriage are the same as the Village. The island's residents police themselves, without outside political or law enforcement influence.

The marriage rituals are the same and the grueling initiation process is a direct replica. The swirling black tattoo Rockland, our leader, designed is inked on each member when they enter the Parrish Brotherhood. I wear one proudly on my own chest. I've seen Charlie eyeing it whenever she gets a chance. She likes it too.

Children coexist with Bachman life; they are sheltered from the more delicate domestic marriage elements, but it's not suburbia. It's a seaside village. The family gathers every Saturday for brunch to celebrate another good week.

In the past, men would travel hundreds of miles to pledge themselves to the Bachman Brotherhood. Carpenters, bankers, gangsters, chefs. Word got around to the other islands, and the Parrish grew and so did their income.

Those men fell in love with the family's way of life.

So did I.

I joined soon after that. Never looked back. I'd do anything for this family.

She'd best stay away. There's too much at stake. And if she knew what we're doing out here...

She'd want off this island as fast as possible.

CHAPTER
THIRTEEN

C harlie

I can't believe I did it again. I let him take control, ravish my body, and this time in his sex dungeon no less. At least this time there was no unprotected sex, so that was responsible... *Yeah, whatever you have to tell yourself to make yourself feel better, you little sex fiend.*

She's an annoying little truth teller. I roll my eyes. Thanks, she-devil.

The evening was wonderful, borderline magical. After our deep conversations about our pasts, I almost feel guilty for crossing him now, going to the boathouse. Not bad enough to hang up my gumshoes, though. I rush up to my room, take a quick shower, then slip into sweats and my sneakers. I pull my hair back into a ponytail.

Wait, I'm wearing all white. Shouldn't I be wearing black? Quickly, I change into black pants and hoodie. Now I'll blend in with the dark night. Much better. This time when I sneak down the stairs, no one stops me.

I slip through the little black door and into the basement, jogging down the secret tunnel. The only sound is the soles of my sneakers as they slap against the ground. My heart is racing hard, pounding in my ears. I'm just waiting to get caught.

Finally, I make it to the exit that leads into the boathouse where we dined tonight. Seeing the boat where we ate together tears another pang of guilt through me. Then I remember the scream, the strange actions of the staff, and I press on. If something funny is going on here, Rockland needs to know. The family deserves to know.

The night air is arctic, the blast of frigid air making me want to crawl back into my four-poster bed, a fire roaring in my fireplace. Well, not my fireplace, per se. Depending on what I find tonight, this may be my last night here at the castle.

I creep down along the shore, staying as close to the tree line as possible. I pop my hood up over my head, hoping for further cover. "Gosh, it's freezing!" I shove my hands in the pockets of my hoodie and jog toward the off-limits boathouse.

There it is!

My heart lurches into my throat as the building comes into view. It's dark, not even an outside light on. I get as close as I can while still feeling like I'm hidden amongst the trees, and I just watch.

I'm turning into a Charlie popsicle when I hear the quiet hum of a motorboat. The boat comes into view, pulling quietly up to the dock by the shore. Holy cow. Something's happening.

In the moonlight, I recognize the driver as the one that first brought me and Nikolaos over to the island, Aiden. He moves quickly, tying the boat to the dock. He jumps back on the boat, pulling a tarp up and over the back of the boat.

My heart stops beating, my breath frozen in my chest. I can't believe what I'm seeing. What on earth is happening...

Aiden is helping people up from where they were hiding underneath the tarp. The shipment he brought over is human. A lineup of women, young, bedraggled women, beautiful and terrified, follows him over to the boathouse.

A light flickers on and the door opens. Nikolaos stands there, having changed out of the suit from earlier, now wearing a casual tee and jeans. My jaw drops as I watch him shut the door behind the string of women.

The cargo. Was. Women.

Is he running some kind of sex trafficking ring out here on Dark Island? I know for a fact the family would be vehemently opposed to something like that. Nikolaos is the newest brother, is there any chance Rockland didn't do a thorough enough investigation before bringing him on board?

It's happened once before... a man infiltrated the family... one who wasn't who or what he said he was.

I will not let it happen again.

I have to get closer to see what's really going on. I sneak over to a window, peeking over the sill. There's a sliver of a crack in the opening of the curtains. I can see into the room, which is small. The girls are huddled together still, looking scared to death. One woman turns toward the window, as if she senses me.

Her eyes trail to the window and I get a good look at her face. Oh my gosh... Her eye is bruised purple underneath, her lip swollen an angry red. I think of the screams I've heard. What have they done to her?

My stomach sinks into the soles of my sneakers. What do I do? There's no way I can just bust in there and help them. Besides, I don't even really know what's going on here.

Maybe... maybe Nikolaos is helping these women?

Then I hear another scream, the same sound I heard the other night. There's no denying it now. It's a woman's scream, and she's in pain. Terror slashes at my heart. I have no idea what to do, how to help. I'm scared and confused. I just need to get out of here. I take off toward the woods.

All my clues flicker through my mind. The secrecy. The boats. The cover of night. The dark island.

I think as I jog back to the other boathouse that houses the riverboat. It's all making sense. He's using this place to traffic vulnerable women. There's no other possible explanation. I just heard a news report about how bad this is getting in the city, how there's a big, powerful ring of men trafficking women, but they've had an impossible time tracking down the criminals, tracing their paths.

I go in the tunnel, running now, so ready to be back in the warmth and safety of my room. My mind whirls. He's probably using the Bachmans' technology to stay undercover, our connections to keep himself under the radar of law enforcement. He's not a beast. He's a monster. I hate myself for sleeping with him. I should have fought him off, turned him down. My God, if he is a monster, there's a chance I'm pregnant by him.

What was I thinking?

I sneak through the castle, going to my room and locking the bedroom door behind me. I dive under the comforter. I can't get the cold to leave my bones. I'm exhausted. Confused. I was drawn to the castle because I was so damn lonely at home. I hated being lonely as a kid, and now, I've gotten myself trapped on this island because I'm weak. I didn't want to be alone again.

What am I going to do?

I don't have my phone. There's no access to a computer here, so no help from Google. I rack my brain trying to remember what I heard in that news story. I think there was mention of the team using a boat to transport the women...

I have to get help. Whatever he's doing in that boathouse, there's no way the family knows about it. He's supposed to be a security guard, for goodness' sake. But I don't want to go to Rockland unless I have more information.

But then I think of the version of the Beast that was sitting across from me at dinner. The talks we had. How highly his staff speak of him. How much Dr. Williams loves him.

He couldn't be capable of something like this, could he?

My past creeps up the back of my neck, circling my mind like a black cloud. I ignored suspicions about a man before and it almost got someone I love killed. I can't ignore what I saw. I need to find out the truth.

I will never, ever be the person who is responsible for having someone hurt this family.

Not again.

I need to confront him. Get the truth out of him. Find a way to interrogate him. He's so much stronger than me, the only way to do this is to flip the power script. I need to be in control of him for once.

What's his weakness? His Achilles heel?

I think hard until the answer hits me.

Me.

I'm his weakness. He gets around me and he can't control himself. I'm going to seduce him, then somehow, lock him up and force him to answer my questions.

There have to be some handcuffs around this place. I'll find them and tell him I want to play, that I like when he's in control, but I want a turn. Then I'll lock his wrists to a bedpost. And I won't let him go till he answers my questions.

I need help. I need Ashely. I pick up the landline on the desk, dialing the number to her office.

She answers with a chipper, "Hello, Charlie! What can I do for you?" Thank goodness she's working late.

"Hey, Ashely. Sorry to bother you, but I was wondering if you could help me gather a few supplies." I ignore the heat that rises in my face as I list off what I want.

Professional to the core, she answers my strange request with, "Yes, ma'am! I'll be right up with all of those items. See you soon."

Twenty minutes later, Ashely is standing at my bedroom door, a discreet black bag hanging from her hands. I thank her, inviting her in.

She sets the bag on the desk and gives it a pat. "Everything you need is right in here. Anything else?"

Nerves make me queasy, but I press forward. I need to ask this question. "Yeah. Just one thing. Um, Ashely?"

"Yes?"

"Quick question."

"Okay…" She smiles. "What is it?"

I take a deep breath, gathering my courage. A beat later I just come out and say it. "Do you know anything about the boathouse?"

A flicker of recognition passes over her face, but she quickly pulls her features back together. "Oh yes! I heard you had the most amazing date there. Dinner on the boat? So romantic—"

I drop my tone. "Not that boathouse, Ashely."

Her face goes dark, her eyes dropping from my face to the toes of her shoes. She's quiet for a moment, thinking of what she's going to say. Finally, she looks back up at me. "I don't know what goes on at the boathouse. But I know enough to know to stay away." She glances pointedly at the black hoodie, sweatpants, and sneakers I left discarded in the armchair by the fire. "And I suggest you stay away too. At all costs."

She knows about my snooping. I don't know what to say...

She brings a false brightness into her glued-on professional smile. "Anything else I can do for you before I turn in for the night?"

Either she really doesn't know anything, or she's scared. I'm not going to push her. I shake my head. "No. Thank you for the... supplies."

"Of course." She shoots me a smile-less wink and a little goodbye waggle of her fingers. "Have fun!"

The moment the door shuts behind her, I get to work.

It's time for Charlie 2.0 to come out and play.

CHAPTER FOURTEEN

Beast
What's this?

My heart thumps once, then twice, then stops, taking a pause before it starts back up again. Miss Charlie Bachman, prim and proper, flowers and pearls, is standing before me wearing...

The sexiest thing I've ever seen in my life.

She's dressed in a black lace corset, her full breasts fighting to be released from it. Black thigh-highs with lace at their tops, garters clipped into the stockings, holding them up. Her perfect pussy is encased in black silk, the first pair of panties I've seen her wear. She's finished off the perfect outfit with what can only be described as high, black fuck-me boots.

In her hand, she holds a pair of silver handcuffs. She twirls one cuff around her bloodred fingernail. She drags the tip of her pink tongue over her glossy red lips and cocks a brow.

"Hey, there." Her eyes lock on mine, and whatever that energy is that exists between us passes through me, hitting me in my core. A slow smile of seduction spreads over her beautiful face. She lifts the handcuffs in the air, dangling them from her finger. "After seeing all those toys in your sex room, I thought you might like to play a little game."

God damn.

But her gaze leaves mine as she makes her way over to me, each step as graceful as a ballerina in those high-heeled boots. I hold back my reaction, my gut clenching as suspicion creeps up my spine. I tell my ever-hardening erection to slow down.

I need time to figure out...

What's this little girl up to?

"Hey, yourself." I take her in, from the sleek new style of her hair to the open toes of those boots, bloodred toenails on toes I suddenly want to put in my mouth and suck on. "What's going on?"

She falters. "What do you mean, what's going on?" Quickly recovering, her voice drops to that kitten purr she first welcomed me with. She arches a brow. "Can't you tell? I'm seducing you."

She stands in the center of the room. I walk around her slowly, taking her in at every angle. My cock isn't ready for the backside of this work of art. The back of the panties she wears are nonexistent, nothing but a thread hidden between her ass cheeks, her curves completely exposed, framed by the buttoned-up back of the corset and the lacy tops of the thigh-highs.

If I had an artist on staff, I'd handcuff her to the wall and have her painted, wanting to have access to this vision forever. I lock this perfect image of her away in my memory, knowing our time together is limited. I should have sent her back already. People are asking me questions, wondering why she's staying here, her friends wanting to know when she'll be back.

Why haven't I sent her back?

She stands perfectly still as she turns her face over her shoulder to look at me. She gives me a little smile, putting on that sexy façade. "You like what you see?" But behind her eyes, I see that fear, that nervous innocence of a woman who's not yet quite fully unleashed her sexuality. I see her desire for acceptance.

I see a scared little girl wanting to be loved.

And that's why I haven't sent her back.

I want to save her.

I want to make her love me.

Jesus, Nikolaos. Where the hell did that come from? Probably from the same place as that feeling of my heart dropping into my gut when she told me that there was no baby.

God, this is fucked up.

But I can't stop.

I reach out, brushing her hair over one shoulder so I can kiss her neck. She shivers as my lips caress her delicate skin. I inhale the sweet scent that is just her, a smell I'm growing all too familiar with.

I'm beginning to crave it.

Her hand reaches back for me, rubbing along the back of my neck. Her touch sends the most amazing tingles over my entire body. I run my fingertips down her other arm, her skin bare and cold in the night air. She gives a soft sigh, leaning into me as I kiss her neck in a way I know marks it as mine.

I circle her wrist, tipping the handcuffs she holds into my hand. She barely notices my movement, she's so entranced by my kisses. She startles, breaking away from me as I clasp the first cuff around her wrist.

Her hand falls from my head as she whips around. "What are you doing?"

"I thought we could play a game," I say, stealing her words from her. I clasp her other wrist in the open cuff.

Her eyes go wide. "What kind of game?"

"A little game where I interrogate you." I run my fingers up her arms, resting my hands on her shoulders as I lock in on her gaze. "And find out exactly what it is you are up to."

"What I'm up to?" She looks away.

"Yes."

I move her toward the bed. She tries to fight me, struggling against me as I lift her arms, unclasping a cuff as I wind the center links around the bedpost then reattach the cuff around her wrist. She stands there, her back against the post, her arms locked behind her back.

Trapped and all mine.

Her gaze goes defiant as she cocks her chin in the air. "Well. What do you want to know?"

I press my fingers against her lips. "I'll ask the questions." I drag my finger from her lip down over the curve of her chin, lighting over her neck, between her breasts, down her trembling stomach till I reach that heavenly patch of silk. The fabric is thin and slippery as I move my fingertip over her pussy.

"Oh…" Her eyes close, her back arching against the post as she shudders lightly.

I tower over her, loving the pink blooming on her cheeks as I stroke her pussy over her panties. "Is there anything you want to tell me? Any special reason you had those cuffs out tonight?"

"I told you…" She gives a little pant. "I just wanted to play."

"It just seems a little out of character for you, to go from trying to run away from me every time I see you to trying to seduce me."

"Well, we had such a nice dinner together earlier. I changed my mind about you."

"Oh, really." I slip the tip of my finger under the elastic band of her panties, finding her warm wetness. I circle her clit with my slickened finger. "And what do you think of me now?"

"Oh. God."

"I'm not God but thank you for the compliment." I drop down on my knees before her.

I stare up at her, holding her gaze as I slip my fingers under the bottom edge of her corset, finding the thin waistband of her panties where they hug her hips. "Look at me," I say, wanting to drink in more of that fear-filled excitement in her eyes.

Slowly, ever so slowly, I peel the panties down from her hips, stopping to unclip those garters from the stockings, leaving them hanging. I slip the panties over her stockings, over those gorgeous fuck-her boots and help her step out of them.

She's shaking as I smooth my hands up her thighs. I grab her soft flesh, parting her legs. Her boots slide apart, and the soft scent of her pussy reaches me, making my mouth water.

I've been dreaming of this moment, of tasting her. I almost regret locking her up, wanting to feel the magical touch of her hands in my hair again. But also, I want her to be completely powerless in this moment.

My gut is telling me there's more to the story. I'm going to enjoy every second of finding out what it is. I dip just the tip of my tongue between the lips of her pussy. I flick it over her clit, and her body ricochets against the bedpost.

"Oh… gosh… that feels incredible."

God. She tastes incredible. Like I knew she would. I want this pussy to belong to me and only me. "How long has it been since a man ate your pussy?"

"Too long. Maybe my honeymoon? Years ago."

While I have her here…

I might as well find out more about her past.

I slip a finger inside of her, adding some friction to go along with the caresses of my warm, wet tongue. "Tell me. How did you first meet the family?"

"My name was Alice. I got a job working part-time… God, that feels good… for Bronson at Bachman's Jewelers, working at the… at the… counter." She gives a gasp, searching for air. "He found me there. Came in one day, looking for a watch. I helped him. We started to date. I thought he loved—" She shudders and moans.

"Keep going, baby." I coax her with my tongue.

"My fiancé was a" —she gives a gasp as I flick at her clit again— "bad man. He was going through initiation to become a brother, but it turns out he was using me to get to the head of the family at the time, Bronson."

I haven't heard this story before. I want to know more. And I want to taste more of that perfect pussy. I lap at her sex, using the flat of my tongue to encourage her to continue her story.

She shudders as she speaks. "He tried to kill Bronson to gain power for the family he worked for. He stabbed him, but Bronson won the fight and killed him. Thank God." I add a second finger to the first, pressing it into her tight pussy as I lick her. She shudders, offering more. "But it took me a long time to trust again."

"And after that, you became Charlie?"

She gives her head a little nod. "Unh... I was so... so ashamed after that. I wanted to become someone else. Leave little loveless Alice behind. I started going by my middle name. I dyed my blonde hair brown."

I pull my mouth away from her sex just long enough to ask, "And your husband?"

"I don't know." She shakes her head. She would have come by now, but my questions make her think and speak and she can't focus solely on the orgasm. I'm drawing it out slowly. "He was the first guy I felt kind of okay around. The Beauties all wanted me to be married, to not be alone. They pressured me and... Oh my God. That feels so... I've never told anyone this, why am I telling you this? I loved him but wasn't in love with him. Oh my... I've never said that out loud, have I?" She gasps as I swirl my fingers inside her. "I was lonely, and he was a good man, the opposite of my fiancé. I guess you could say...he was a safe bet."

I pump my fingers inside of her, stroking her clit with the pad of my thumb. I stare up at her face, so beautiful, so tortured. "Then what happened?"

"He died on our honeymoon. A diving accident."

My hand stills. "And you've been alone ever since?"

"That's why I don't date. I'm cursed." Her words go to a whisper as she glances down at me. The pain in her eyes makes that strange tugging in my chest return. "I don't want to lose another one."

I slip my fingers from her. I want to make that pain go away.

I grab her thighs. "Thank you. For telling me." And I bury my face in that gorgeous pussy of hers, eating her out. She calls my name, "Nikolaos!" Her breaths gasp in hard, shuddering bursts as she comes.

I keep going.

"Oh my God. I can't take anymore—"

I lap at her clit, keeping a steady rhythm. Her hips start to gyrate, moving in time with my tongue. A whine rises from her as she rides the wave of a second climax. Her entire body tightens into one tense muscle, then the sweet release hits her and she cries out. Her body crumples against the bedpost.

"And the handcuffs?" I ask.

"I wanted an explanation of what I saw in the boathouse tonight." She glances down at me, giving me a sheepish smile. "I was supposed to be interrogating you."

"You've been such a good girl. Telling me the truth." I stand, leaning over her, pressing my body against hers as I reach behind her to unlock the cuffs. I press a little silver button. One she could have very easily pressed herself to get free. I reach behind her head, slipping my fingers through her hair. My mouth finds hers, locking us in a deep kiss. When I pull away, she's breathless.

"Get dressed and I'll show you what you want to see."

CHAPTER
FIFTEEN

Beast

It's freezing out here. Two a.m. I made her put on a couple of layers as well as one of my coats. It's too big on her, swallowing her up and making her look positively tiny, but it's keeping her warm. She's clinging to me, her arms wrapped around one of mine, her hand small in mine. She's scared, but she trusts me. I can feel it. A newfound sense of responsibility washes over me. I brought her here. I'm the only one who can protect her, keep her safe...

Make her happy.

First, I have to show her what I've been hiding.

"Tell me what you saw in your spying," I request, leading her down the dimly lit path.

"I saw the guy that brought us over drive up in a boat. He pulled a tarp back. And there were women on the boat." She gives me a nervous glance, her trust wavering as she continues. "Then, I saw one of the girls in the room. She was in bad shape. She looked like she'd been… hit."

"She had. All the woman on my boats have been hurt. The scream you heard the other night? That was Dr. Williams popping a dislocated shoulder back into place. She's often setting bones, giving stitches."

"Oh my." Her hand squeezes mine.

"That first room you saw was just our intake room. We do a quick count, a brief assessment of injuries, then we take them into the actual boathouse."

"Where are they coming from?" she asks. "What are they doing here?"

My throat gets tight, thinking of what we're doing here. "I can't tell you. But I can show you that they are alright. That we are taking good care of them."

"Okay. I don't understand, but I appreciate you showing me that the girls I saw are really okay."

They aren't okay, they never will be, not really. They'll carry their pain with them for the rest of their lives, but hopefully, now, they are safe.

I press my finger on the security keypad at the back of the building, which is actually now the front door. No one gets in other than the girls and my small team of trusted associates. The door opens, leading us into a foyer. There's another door for added protection of the women. I unlock that one the same way and push the door open. A soft glow fills the foyer.

"Go ahead." I let go of her hand, gesturing for her to go first. It might be two a.m., but there's no way the women are asleep yet.

Dr. Williams will still be seeing after them, and then they tend to like to take hour-long showers.

She steps into the boathouse, offering a timid, "Hello?"

Twelve sets of curious eyes look up at her from their various places in the room. I've tried to make the room as comfortable as possible, filling it with several daybeds and couches where the women can rest, but still be together. None of them want to be isolated or alone after what they've just been through.

Charlie receives a few waves, a few shy greetings. Dr. Williams is seated next to a young woman, holding a stethoscope to her chest.

She looks up in surprise, then shoots me a glance of admonishment. "I knew you had a soft spot for this Charlie girl, but bringing her in here? Is that really a good idea?"

"Hello, Dr. Williams," Charlie says, politely. "Good to see you again."

"Good to see you too, honey. Even under these strange circumstances." The doctor looks back to me. "How much have you told her?"

"Nothing. And I'll keep it that way." I glance down at Charlie. "But she saw the girls arrive and I wanted her to know they are safe and in good hands."

Dr. Williams nods. "I understand. But not a word of this to anyone, Charlie. Do you understand? It's for their safety."

Charlie nods. "Yes, ma'am. I understand. I just needed to see them." Charlie gives me a grateful look, then to my surprise, leaves my side. She shrugs out of my coat, carefully folding and draping it over the back of a chair.

She goes over to one of the beds where the youngest woman in this shipment sits alone, shivering. I think the name she gave us was

Pippa. Charlie grabs a quilt that's folded at the foot of the bed. Moving carefully, she unfolds the blanket, gently wrapping it around the girl's shoulders. Then she sits next to the girl, wrapping her arms around her, and just holds her.

The young woman's features hold steady for a moment, trying to be strong, but with a gentle word from Charlie and a tightening of her hug, the young woman's face crumples. She buries her face into Charlie's clavicle. Giant sobs wrack her slight shoulders. Charlie holds her, whispering soft words, smoothing down her dark hair, and just lets her cry.

"It's okay. It's going to be okay. You're safe now." Charlie's eyes look for mine. She holds them, giving me a small nod.

She trusts me.

And I trust her. I can sense that she knows the last thing these women need right now is someone prying. And with Dr. Williams clearly telling her to mind her business, I have no doubts that Charlie will hold to that.

I thought if Charlie saw these women, she might want to run back to her perfect life in the city. She's done the opposite, diving right in to help. I should have known she would. I step outside, leaving Charlie to tend to the girls.

I need to call Rockland with an update.

He answers on the first ring. We shoot the shit, and I give him the update. Then I tell him about taking Charlie to the boathouse. It was unavoidable.

"How much does she know?" he asks.

"She knows that we bring the girls here by boat under the cover of darkness. That we keep them under lock and key at the boathouse.

That they come to us hurt, that Dr. Williams is working with us, that we are keeping them safe."

"And she knows better than to pry any further," he says. "I know Charlie. She wouldn't do anything to hurt this family. She'll keep it to herself. You want to tell me why you took her in the first place?"

"She was pregnant with my baby. But it didn't work out. I wanted Dr. Williams to look at her. She's fine, but she hasn't told anyone in the family what happened." I'm speaking on behalf of Charlie. She'd kept everything to herself, so I can only assume I'm right in saying, "We'd like to keep it that way."

"Understood. And now?" he asks.

Now? I can't let her leave. "I'm going to keep her here for a while longer."

He says, "I think that's our best bet, considering what we're trying to pull off out there."

"Can you hold the Beauties off?" I ask. "Keep them at bay a little while longer?"

"Yeah." He gives a gruff laugh. "I'll just have Tess tell them you two are on your honeymoon. That's what she thinks, anyway."

"That's not funny."

He laughs again. "It is to me. Tess called it when she saw you watch Charlie walk into a room the first time you saw her. Tess is never wrong."

"We'll see," I say, my voice sounding tight.

When I come back into the room, Charlie's painting Pippa's nails. The girl's tears are dried and there's a smile on her face. Charlie sees me enter the room and whispers something to Pippa. Pippa gives me a shy glance and quickly looks back to Charlie, giggling.

It's three in the morning. I've got to get Charlie some rest. I pry her away from Pippa. She doesn't want to go but she's exhausted. She gives the girl a long hug and plants a kiss on the top of her head. "I'll come see you tomorrow. I promise. Careful, your nails are still wet."

I help her back into my coat. "It's cold out there."

I give Charlie a quick tour of the rest of the boathouse on the way out. We installed private showers like the ones in the guestrooms of the castle, each one fully stocked with high-end haircare, skincare, and beauty products. Anything to help these women feel human again.

We have a huge room of clothes, shoes, and accessories we collected from the Beauties' last clothing drive. They thought the goods were being shipped to a shelter in the city. Everything actually came here instead. It was the easiest way to get clothing and shoes of all different sizes and the women seem to love picking out items from the "closet." Charlie sees a purple and black floral dress she recognizes as hers.

"I have more. I can get you more of everything, anything you need," she offers as we step out into the night.

"I think we're good." I think of Pippa's giggles. I'm curious. "What did you tell that girl about me?"

"I told her that they call you the Beast." She glances up at me. "But that it turns out you're just a big, toasted marshmallow. A little burnt on the outside but sweet on the inside."

"Oh, really? Is that how you see me? A giant marshmallow?"

"You're so big. I'm sure after whatever they've been through, you look super scary. I didn't want her to be afraid of you." She nudges my ribs. "Besides. It's true. You do have a sweet side."

"Can we just keep that between us? Please."

"Your secret is safe with me." The teasing leaves her voice as she catches my eye. "And I want you to know, your other secret is safe with me too. I don't have any idea what you are doing here, but I know you are helping those women. And I know whatever is going on, you're working hard to keep their location a secret to keep them safe. I'll keep your secret."

"I trust you."

"And I want to help, in any way I can. It's amazing how something small like a manicure can make someone feel better. I know I can't do much, but I can do the little things. Help them with their hair, or nails, or feed them. There's this casserole I make whenever someone's having a tough time. You know—that kind of meat and potatoes comfort food people crave in hard times. And first thing in the morning I'm putting in an order with Lush to have chocolates shipped here. They're open 24 hours, which I love, in case anyone has a chocolate emergency, for which I think this situation definitely qualifies." She gives me a shy look, careful not to overstep. "If that's okay with you, that is. And if you think they'd like something like that."

She's so fucking sweet. My voice goes gruff. "That'll be fine. What girl doesn't like chocolate?"

"Exactly." She looks up at me, her face bursting into a smile. "You get it."

And there it is, that burning, yearning in my chest.

Am I falling for her?

Or have I already fallen, tipping over the edge of a cliff the moment I laid eyes on her?

I take her back to her room. She makes her call to Lush over speakerphone as she gets undressed. I stand and stare, enjoying every glimpse I get of her beautiful body as she tugs on her pajamas. I want to rip them back off, scoop her up in my arms and carry her to my bed. Ravage her. Kiss and lick and touch every inch of her. Take my time with her, time I didn't have earlier tonight in the dungeon.

But that's not what she needs. What she needs is sleep. I tuck her into bed. She's exhausted, her eyes fluttering. I'll go back to my room tonight, let her sleep. I lean down, placing a chaste kiss on her cheek. She purrs at my touch.

The theme for the night seems to be truth telling. I have one more truth bomb to drop on her. I push her hair back from her face as she closes her eyes. I lean down, my lips brushing her soft earlobe.

"Now that you know, I can't let you leave."

CHAPTER SIXTEEN

Charlie

It's obvious what he's undertaken here on his island. He's not operating a human trafficking ring.

He's the leader of a movement risking everything to destroy one.

And now, I'm an accomplice.

I can't leave.

I wouldn't do anything to put those women further into harm's way. Nikolaos and Rockland are concerned that if I leave the island, the secret could somehow leave with me. Or, God forbid, be drawn from me. These are bad men, the worst of the worst, running this ring. Who knows what kind of spies they have out in the world?

I'm safer here. The women are safer if I stay. Besides, I want to help. And I'm no longer afraid of the Beast. It turns out Nikolaos isn't only a Greek god. He's a superhero.

Which complicates my already confused myriad of thoughts.

When there was a chance he was a bad dude, it was easy to convince myself I should be staying away from him. But now? After getting glimpses of the real him, his softer side, hearing about his past, and finding out he's trying to save the world...

I've no reason to stay away from him.

But it's not my castle.

And he's not my man.

So, one would say I should keep to myself.

But I'm me, Charlie Bachman. I can't hear someone's having a bad day without baking a casserole. I'm not going to be able to stay away from that boathouse. I know that about myself.

What I wouldn't have guessed about myself is that I can't stay away from him. I'd sworn off men. I'd promised my cursed little self that I'd never date again. But here I am, perfectly happy with the fact I can't leave. I blame it on that little she-devil living on my shoulder. That and the throbbing in my core that starts to hum like a heartbeat every time the darn man gets within arm's reach of me.

He's having all my clothing and personal effects shipped here from my townhouse in a few days. He said it's not forever, just for now, and he wants me to be comfortable. I lack for nothing. When the shipments of chocolates I'd ordered for the girls came in with the sun this morning, there were three extra boxes of assorted pieces with my name on them.

And one bar of milk chocolate. Its tag read, *For little Alice, as sweet as chocolate and strong as stone.*

Courtesy of him.

He'd called up Lush and tacked the items onto my order. It's enough chocolate to last me months, especially now that I'm no longer alone, buried under blankets and tissues, crying on my couch.

I slip my favorite, a milk chocolate filled with creamy caramel, between my lips. I'm never alone here. And I'm not unhappy.

I'm... happy. I have been since I arrived on this whirlwind of an adventure. A little confused by my emotions and desires, sure. There were a few harrowing moments when I thought Nikolaos was a sex trafficker, yes.

Have I experienced moments of white-hot shame and self-hatred?

Of course.

But the sexcapades were magnificent. The dinner date—was it a *date,* date? —was the most fun I've had in a long time, connecting one on one with another person over delicious food and wine, in an incredibly romantic atmosphere. Meeting Dr. Williams, who calmed my fears. Being involved in helping women who desperately need to see a kind face. The exciting adventure of staying in a castle.

With a real-life Beast.

This kidnapping has lifted me out of my dark cloud, giving me hope for better days to come. Will those days be with him by my side while I stay here? Time will tell. I have no idea what to expect. I only know I'm feeling drawn to that boathouse and I'm going to chase that feeling.

I dress comfy but take more time on my hair and makeup than I care to admit, even adding a splash of perfume before I walk out the door. I head down to the kitchen where Remy waits for me.

This morning, the two of us are making the girls crepes. He's been in on what's been happening at the boathouse as he's been cooking for our guests. We'll fill the crepes with fresh fruit and serve them with several protein options that Remy was already planning on, to help refuel their energy after their journey.

It's too dangerous to have the women come to the castle to dine, so I've gotten Nikolaos's permission to set up an empty room in the back of the boathouse as a dining room. For now, it's just a few folding tables and chairs we found in the back of the basement, but later today, I'll be calling all my favorite stores in the city to put in an order. By the end of the week, the boathouse will have its own dining room. While Remy finishes up with the cooking, I excuse myself to go to the greenhouse. I carefully cut bouquets of the orange mums and pink treasure flowers I spied the other day, to pretty up my card tables for breakfast.

Remy let me snoop around the butler's pantry, pulling linens and tableware for what I'm now calling in my head the Welcome Breakfast. Pippa helps me spread the brightly colored floral-patterned tablecloths I found in the back of a drawer over the tables.

We arrange the orange and pink blooms in plastic vases that were easier to carry over than the gorgeous heavy cut glass vases he's got in his butler's pantry. Pippa's arrangement is gorgeous. "You have an eye for this," I tell her. "You're a natural."

She gives me a shy smile. "Thanks. I actually grew flowers before—" Her sentence cuts off. They've been instructed not to share anything personal with me for their safety.

"Flowers are healing, aren't they?" I wrap an arm around her thin shoulders. "Come on, let's go see if Remy's here with the food."

I stand back as the women eat, refilling their water and juice glasses. It feels good to serve. Afterward, the women thank me with hugs, the more timid ones with small smiles. I know Remy has his plate full—chef pun? —so I send him back to the kitchen and do the clearing up on my own.

I spend the rest of the day offering the women manicures. I keep the small talk light and impersonal, or sometimes we don't talk at all, just listen to the soft music I've now got piping through the room from a speaker I had Nikolaos install after breakfast. He didn't even bat an eye when I asked him for the favor. He just made it happen.

Not gonna lie. I really liked that. And I'm not going to lie about how sexy he looked, standing on that step stool, hanging the speaker up in the corner, the olive-toned expanse of his lower back showing as he raised his muscular arms overhead for the installation.

And the way his ass looks in his jeans…he could be my handyman any day. My little she-devil says, *He could hammer into me any day.*

I go about my day, ordering the furniture as well as a few articles of clothing we were short on. When early evening rolls in, I figure it's the perfect time to drop by the boathouse with my offerings of chocolate.

It's quiet when I step into the room. "Hello?" My voice echoes back to me.

I'm all alone. The boathouse is empty.

The girls are gone.

.

CHAPTER
SEVENTEEN

Beast

When Charlie comes dashing down the hall of the castle, looking for me, I know exactly why she's here. I grab her shoulders, grounding her as she catches her breath. "Whoa, there, little lady. Slow down."

"The girls—" She sucks in a deep breath. "Where are the girls?"

I want nothing more than to sit down with her, tell her everything. She became so invested in such a short amount of time. I know this is killing her. I wrap my arms around her waist. Like she's mine.

I look down at her, apologies in my tone. "You know I can't tell you anything. I'm sorry."

She gives me a pleading look. Those hazel eyes make a zing of energy burst through my heart whenever she locks her gaze on mine. She shakes her head, the end of her long ponytail swinging gently.

"Just tell me they're safe," she says.

"They are. They're safe." For now.

We've gotten word the leaders of the ring have suspicions about me, about Dark Island. We decided the best thing to do now is to keep the women on the island for the shortest amount of time possible before moving them on to another safe house. This time, the girls were here for less than 24 hours.

We've been doing this for months, saving almost one hundred women. With this new information, I'm not sure how much longer we'll be able to bring them to the island, and I'm uneasy running the operation with Charlie here.

I don't want to do anything to put her at risk. There are eyes and ears everywhere. Theirs, and ours. The family is sending more equipment and manpower for added security for the island, but that will only keep the people living here safe. If they find out where we are, the added safety measures won't be enough to get the boats here from the lake.

The family leaders are putting our heads together tonight to decide how to move forward. I've got a lot of phone calls and meeting plans ahead of me. But right now? All I want to do is focus on Charlie.

She poses her question like a statement. "And you can't tell me any more than that?"

"Correct."

"I get it." Her gaze falls to the floor as she nods, biting her bottom lip. Her eyes shift back up to mine. "Doesn't mean I'm not going to worry about them."

I wrap an arm around her shoulders. "I know. I get it. But tell you what, it's out of our hands for now. Let's try to enjoy the peace. How about having dinner with me again tonight?"

She sighs softly. "I could eat. And last night was…" Her voice gets quiet, shy. "Special."

I slip a little packet from my pocket. I'd put it there this morning and carried it with me all day. I have something in my other pocket too, in case I find a need for it later.

"I have something for you." I hand her the little silver sachet.

"What's this?" She takes the little package, her eyes glittering as she opens it. Her mouth forms a little "o" of surprise as she opens the gift. "Oh my gosh. This is for me? You're too sweet."

She holds the pendant in her hand. It's a little glass circle framed in silver, hanging from a silver chain. Inside is a tiny, pressed flower, its petals still bright white after all these years, its center a golden yellow like the sun. I don't know what possessed me to grab the necklace from the collection I inherited when I first bought the castle, but I did.

It just looked like Charlie. She's as cheerful as a flower and when she walks in a room, she warms me. Like I'm stepping into the sun. Jesus, what's happening to me? I clear my throat, willing the obsessive Charlie thoughts to leave my brain.

"Sweet," I say. "That's not a word that's been used to describe me before."

"I told you, you're all gooey inside like a marshmallow." She hands me the necklace, pulling her hair off her neck for me to put it on her. Why do I like the small gesture so much, that she didn't just put it on herself, but turned to me to do the honors?

I close the delicate clasp, resting it on the back of her neck.

She turns to show me, her fingers going to the pendant.

"I love, love, love it. Thank you." She reaches up on tiptoe, planting a sweet little kiss on my cheek. Even that, the tiny gesture of a thank you kiss...

My chest burns.

"It looks beautiful on you." Like it was always meant to hang around her neck.

I take her hand, leading her to the garden. I had my staff set up a simple dinner in the center of the greenhouse. I hold the door open for her. As she steps inside, she gives a little gasp that lets me know my stellar staff has once again come through for me. The glass roofing has been strung with large white globe lights, their soft glow the only light against the dark night sky that surrounds us.

Dr. Williams called earlier with the results of Charlie's blood tests. I figure it's information best shared face-to-face, so I invited her to have dinner with me again tonight. I tell myself it's just to give her the results, but I know I'm craving that connection we had at our boat dinner.

"I thought you'd like to dine surrounded by flowers."

She glides over to the table like she's walking on water. She lets her fingers trail over the white tablecloth as she takes in the elaborate floral centerpiece on the table. She leans in, taking a deep breath, fully enjoying the over-the-top bouquet.

I just stand by the door and watch her. I love the way she moves, the way she smiles. The way she takes her time to enjoy something she loves, like when she's savoring one of her precious pieces of chocolate.

Finally, her gaze finds mine. "Thank you. So much. This is..." she struggles to find the words. "Incredible."

I pull out a chair for her. "I want to keep my prisoner happy."

She slides into the seat, the smile on her face making me think she's as content as can be to be under my lock and key. The knowledge that I have her, here, all to myself, and she is completely powerless to leave, makes my cock warm in my jeans. I like that she's under my thumb, under my control.

But most of all—under my protection.

I take the seat across from her, pouring her some of the crisp white wine from the chilled bottle. We dine on the meal Remy prepared for us, both of us too focused on our food to chat. Once we've gotten some food in our bellies, I broach the subject I brought her here to cover.

"Dr. Williams called me this afternoon. She got your test results in."

"Oh." She dabs her mouth delicately with the corner of her napkin, then lays it back down on her lap. "Tell me." She shakes her head, holding her hand out to stop me like she's had a second thought. She grabs her wineglass. "No. Wait. Let me finish this first. Liquid courage."

She tips her glass back, draining the wine.

I hold the bottle out. "More?"

She hands me her glass. "Hit me."

I fill her glass back up. She takes another long sip, then sets her glass back down on the tabletop, folding her hands in her lap. "Okay. I'm ready."

I speak quickly, not wanting to leave her in suspense. "Everything looked great. And your DNA test came back clear too. Dr. Williams is happy to meet with you tomorrow to go over everything in person, but she didn't want to keep you waiting. She said to reassure you that what happened was a one-time thing, a fluke."

Her voice is quiet. "It didn't feel like a fluke."

Wrong choice of words? "She doesn't think it will happen again." Which leads me to the question that's been burning in the back of my mind all evening. "Would you want to try? Again? Is having a baby something you want?"

Are those tears shining in her eyes? She blinks a few times, collecting her thoughts or emotions, maybe both. "More than anything in this world. I've always wanted to be a mom. I don't hold my mother's terrible mothering against her, I think she did her best, but even from a young age, I knew I wanted to be a mom, and that if I got to have a child of my own, they would be the most loved, well-cared-for baby in this world."

I'm blown away by how honest she's being, by how much she's sharing.

"And marriage?"

"Nooo..." She shakes her head, her reaction decided and immediate. "Nuh-uh. No way."

She feels very strongly about both topics. I'm just surprised it wasn't yes to both. I took her as more traditional than this. First comes marriage, then the baby in the baby carriage. What's stopping her?

I top off her wine, wanting to extend the conversation, to get more out of her. "Why no to marriage?

"You've heard about my past. You know I've been burned before. First, by a fiancé who was trying to hurt the family. And I didn't see it. I can't believe I didn't see it. And it almost got someone I loved hurt. I couldn't trust after that."

She sips more wine.

"And..."

"And then my husband." She holds my gaze for a beat. "You know what happened to him. He died too. On our honeymoon. That's just crazy. Isn't it?"

I guess it makes sense she doesn't want to marry again, after what she's been through. Still, she just seems like the kind of woman who would want motherhood and marriage to go hand-in-hand. "Do you think things might change over time, that you could ever try it again?"

She shrugs. "I can't."

"Why not?"

"I'm convinced..." She sips a little more wine and gives a tipsy giggle. "I'm cursed."

"Cursed." I remember her saying something about that when I was interrogating her, eating her sweet pussy. I thought it was just an offhand comment. Didn't think she was being serious. And I was a little distracted at that moment.

"Yes." She nods. "Cursed. The common denominator of their deaths? Me. I'm just bad luck. I'm destined to be alone. I don't want to risk losing another man. No, thank you."

"I don't believe in that kind of thing. Sometimes, bad shit just happens. That's life."

"Buuut..." She twists the stem of her wineglass between her forefinger and thumb. "When that bad stuff happens *twice*, you can't just explain it away. It's a curse."

There's no changing her mind. I shift to another subject, trying to keep the mood light. "How many little brats are you thinking of having?"

"You mean, how many precious children am I hoping for?" She gives another giggle. "I don't know. Two? I know myself and I like everything so perfect all the time, I think two might be all I could handle."

"I think you, Charlie Bachman, can handle anything you put your mind to."

My compliment makes her flush. "Thank you. That's sweet."

There's that word again. I raise a brow to her. "Stop calling me sweet or you're going to find yourself over my knee."

She looks right at me, her eyes shining with mischief and wine. "You, Nikolaos Bachman, are a big, sweet, sweetie."

Challenge accepted, little lady.

CHAPTER EIGHTEEN

Charlie

The wine feels good, cruising through my veins, warming my blood. Makes me feel a little bit naughty. My she-devil gives a tipsy laugh, ready to see where this night goes. He tells me I could do anything I put my mind to. How sweet is that? I tell him so.

He lifts a dark brow sky high. "Stop calling me sweet or you're going to find yourself over my knee."

His response makes my blood heat. My two glasses of liquid courage swell my confidence. I want to challenge him. To see what he'll do. I toss a test out into the air, letting it land. "You, Nikolaos Bachman, are a big, sweet, sweetie." And I take another drink of wine.

Let the chips fall where they may.

He pushes his chair back from the table. My pussy gets wet just watching him spread those massive thighs of his. He lifts a finger in the air, crooks it, and beckons me.

"Come. Here."

His low tone rumbles through me. My stomach flip-flops and my knees go to jelly. He wants me to get up, walk over there, and then... what?

He pats his right thigh with that big hand of his. "Now."

Oh dear. What have I gotten myself into? My little she-devil prods me along with the prongs of her pitchfork. I find myself standing, slowly moving toward him in a dreamlike state. Is this really happening? Am I going to consent to this? And where will this lead...

My body obeys as my mind trips over a myriad of nervous thoughts. I take one shaky step toward him. Then a second before pausing as the heat in his gaze burns into me, my belly fluttering. He pats his thigh with his hand one more time, and that hand just looks... so... massive.

I glance at the door, glance back at him, and make my decision. I'm making a break for it.

He senses my move before I make it. He leans up from his seat, grabbing my arm and pulling me to him. He tips me over his lap, wrapping a big arm around my waist, locking me against the hard plane of his belly. The heat from his body envelops me as he curls his body around mine.

"You have such a gorgeous ass." He smooths his palm over my backside. "And now I get to spank it. Lucky me."

I hold in a moan. How do I keep letting myself get into these shamefully sexy situations with him? His hand comes down in a hard spank, and the sting reminds me, I didn't let this happen.

He orchestrates every single moment of our sexcapades. He's in control and I'm powerless and that's the way he likes it. My pussy slickens with arousal. If I'm being honest, it's the way I like it too. I'm beginning to crave his dominance.

His hand comes down again. I suck in air between my teeth as the sting spreads over my other ass cheek. He tugs at the waistband of my stretchy leggings, pulling them down under the curve of my ass. He gives a low whistle, obviously loving what he sees. He smooths his hand over bare skin, his touch leaving behind a trail of tingles. "Ask me to spank you."

Is he… serious? My head flips over my shoulder, trying to find his face. "What?"

He gives my ass a hard squeeze, his fingers digging into my soft flesh. "You heard me."

"Oh, gawd." I can't do this. I hang my head back down. My throat feels tight, my tongue goes numb in my mouth. He gives me another squeeze. The pain makes me choke out the words he demands from me. "Please. Spank me."

"Good girl. You're making me hard." As if on cue, his cock rouses against my belly. I get wetter, knowing how turned on he is. He gives me another spank, then a growl. "I can't wait any longer. I want to punish your ass."

Isn't that what we just did? What more does he have in mind? Nerves flow through me as he snaps my leggings back into place and grabs my hips. He stands me back up, facing him, wedging me between his rock-hard thighs. Holding one of my hands, he slips his other in a pocket.

I stare down at him, heat flushing over my face at the admonishing look he gives me.

"The necklace wasn't the only thing I slipped in my pocket earlier." He pulls a bullet-shaped object and tiny tube of lube from his pocket. "I wanted to be prepared in case your naughty side came out tonight. Not gonna lie. I had my fingers crossed that it would."

He holds up the hot pink object. It's a butt plug. My ass involuntarily clenches. I gulp down my nerves.

"You know exactly what this is. I can see it in your face. And you know just where I'm going to put it." He twists it between his finger and thumb. "But do you know why I'm doing it?"

"To punish me?"

"To prepare that perfect little ass of yours to take all of my cock one day soon."

I glance down at his crotch region, thinking of his massive size. "Nuh-uh. No way. That thing is not going to fit inside of me."

"You mean, my giant cock isn't going to fit in your tight little ass?"

"That's what I said."

"Don't get sassy or I'll fill your mouth with my cock while I fill your ass with my bullet."

I give a gulp.

"Take off your pants. No need to tell you to take off your panties—I know you're not wearing any, naughty girl—and get down on all fours on the ground."

"Haven't seen you wear anything under your jeans, either," I mumble, glancing down at the soft grass, trying to decide if I'm going to obey.

The pad of his thumb slides over my bottom lip. "Still want to be sassy?" He slips his thumb between my lips, sliding it in and out just like he did with his cock that night in the alleyway.

I'm already overwhelmed by the thought of him touching my ass, pushing something inside of me. I shake my head, not wanting to take on more. I answer him, my words mumbled with his thumb filling my mouth.

I try to say "no, sir" but it comes out as, "No, th—thir."

He likes my shame, a wicked grin crossing his handsome face. "Good girl. Now get down on your knees."

My fingers shake as I tug at the waistband of my leggings, pulling them down. Yeah, I'm not wearing panties and the cooler night air rushes over my bare skin. I slip off my sneakers and socks, kick off my pants.

I stand with my feet sinking into the soft grass, wearing a sweatshirt and nothing else. I feel ridiculous, yet there's a thrumming of nervous energy running through my body. What will this feel like? Will it hurt? Will I like it?

Everything he's ever done to me has left me reaching heaven and seeing stars, and that knowledge is really the thing that finally moves me forward. His gaze is heavy on me, watching every movement as I lower my half-naked body to the ground at his feet.

My hands and knees sink into the soft earth, my skin protected from the dirt by the thick, lush grass. The ground and the air are cool, the temperature making the tiny hairs on my arms stand on end. A shiver runs down my spine, from the chill or from his eyes on me, I can't tell.

"Like this?" I ask, wanting to be compliant after his threats.

"Yes, baby. Just like that." His voice is gravelly and sexy, a rake over hot coals.

It's the first time he's called me baby. Not gonna lie. I like it. His words make my pussy get wetter than it already is. I shift my weight from knee to knee, clenching my sex, the desire there beginning to build.

"Dip your fingers inside your pussy and see how wet you already are for me. And I haven't even touched your pussy yet."

I toss him a glance over my shoulder, taking in the way he's sitting in that chair, slung back, legs spread, power oozing from him. I want to snap back with something sassy, dig my fingernails into some shred of dignity and cling to it, but he's too intimidating.

I have to obey.

I draw a shuddering breath, willing my hand to reach between my thighs. Shame fills me, white hot and gut wrenching. I slip my fingers there and goodness knows I'm dripping wet for him. A humiliating moan escapes my lips as I push two of my fingers inside of me. The fullness, the friction only leaves me wanting more, wanting him.

"Good girl. Hold it right there. Don't move those fingers."

I feel him coming closer, kneeling in the grass behind me. It's not lost on me that my ass is on full display for him, but I try not to think about it, instead concentrating on holding my fingers still.

I hear the cap to the lube. He presses his big, warm hand into my lower back. "Keep breathing, baby."

I take a few breaths. The tip of his slick plug pushes against my ass. It's so tight I have to remind myself to keep breathing as he pushes it harder, the tip of it pressing past my unwilling muscles.

"Now, take those wet fingers and pleasure yourself. Rub your clit while I fuck your ass with my plug."

"Oh gawd." I pant, my eyes closed, my head hanging down as I rub my clit. The touch sends a bolt of energy through my body. He pushes the bullet further in, slowly, pulling it back out, slowly. He's gentle at first, then his thrusting grows faster, harder.

Just like he promised, he's fucking my ass with his toy.

His voice rumbles through me, his hand circling my lower back. "This plug has a little extra to it."

"Oh yeah?" I gasp. What could it be?

There's a click and a buzz and all of a sudden, my entire ass is vibrating. "Oh my God!" My back arches, my finger freezing in place as I fight to figure out what's happening to me.

The vibrations from the toy give me feelings I've never experienced. It's so strange, making me feel like I have to pee and come all at the same time. My pussy clenches, empty, begging for some kind of friction and fullness there, and I slip my fingers inside it as my full ass hums with the vibrations.

It all happens so fast, the stimulation overwhelming. My body tightens, clenches, my heart skipping a beat. I feel like I'm going to implode.

"Oh my gosh, I'm going to come. Nikolaos, I'm coming."

He gives my ass a slap, the sting spreading over my skin. "Come for me, babygirl. There's a good girl."

The fingers of the hand supporting me dig into the grass, dirt pressing under my nails. My mouth falls open, my eyes shut tight. White stars blind my vision as a deep moan leaves my chest. I rub my fingers over my clit, and I feel like I'm freefalling, tumbling through the starry night. My body contracts, my ass locking around the toy.

The orgasm comes from so deep within me, I choke on my cry as I climax. "Nik—Nik—Nikolaos!"

He pulls the toy from my ass. I'm recovering, trying to come back to Earth. I feel the lubed head of his cock pressing against the twitching muscles of my ass. "What? Now? You meant now?"

"I can't wait. You're too fucking sexy. I have to take your tight little ass right now." He grabs my hips, pulling me into him as he presses the head of his cock harder against me. "Breathe, baby. Breathe and take my cock."

His palm flattens against my lower back. I take a deep breath, but it doesn't prepare me for the feeling of him plunging the full length of his cock in my ass. I lean forward, my jaw falling open. I'm so full, I feel like I'll burst. He thrusts his cock into me, and I feel it all the way in my chest.

"How does that feel, baby? How does it feel having my cock in your tight little ass?" he growls, rubbing circles over my back. His other hand slips around my waist, finding my clit and playing with it.

"Oh! It hurts... you're so big... it burns... but it feels... oh my God... it feels *gooood*." My fingernails dig into the grass. It feels strange, different from anything I've felt before. I'm so full, he's so deep, the climax beginning to tighten my core is so intense.

"Come for me again, babygirl. Come so hard for me." His fingers work my clit, his cock filling my ass. My world goes black, those white stars coming back. I can't breathe, can't think, the climax tearing through me, my heart racing, perspiration prickling at my skin.

He comes, filling my ass with his hot semen. The naughtiness of it tips me over the edge again, throwing me into yet another orgasm. I come so hard I hear angels knocking on the gates of heaven. *Knock, knock, knock.* I reach out and grab ecstasy, celestial pleasure washing over every inch of my body and...

"Shit. Someone's at the door." His voice brings me back to Earth.

"What? Seriously?" I scramble to my feet on shaky legs, hiding behind the tall branches of a flowering bush.

He tosses me my pants. "Put those on. I'll be right back." He pauses for a moment, his eyes glazed over as he takes me in. "God damn, you're sexy."

I give a giggle. "Go. Go!" I push a foot through a leg of my leggings, hopping on one foot trying to get my other leg in. I'm wet and sticky but I do my best, pulling my shirt down as far as it will go.

"I'm going. But know this, I'm not done with you yet. Later, I want your pussy, too." He shoves his cock in his pants, refastening his belt. He gives me a wicked grin as he turns on his bootheel to go see who's interrupted us.

I hear Ashely's sweet voice. Always the professional, you couldn't tell from her tone whether she suspects anything is going on. "Hello, Mr. Bachman. I am so sorry to interrupt you during your dinner, but we've had a call from the mainland. From the Village. It's an emergency."

"Okay, I'll be right there."

"The call isn't for you." She clears her throat, speaking louder, knowing I'm hiding somewhere in the greenhouse. "The call came in for Miss Charlie. The person said it was urgent."

My heart stops as I slip on my second shoe. What on earth could have happened? I rush to the door.

"Ashely? Who is it?"

"They wouldn't say. They just kept asking for you. They were upset and kind of hard to understand." She grabs my hand. "Come with me. I'll take you to the library where you can have some privacy."

"Thanks." I glance at Nikolaos as I leave. "I'll see you later?"

He gives a nod. "I've got some calls to make."

Knowing him and our family and how quickly word spreads, he'll know what's going on at the same time I do, if not before. The men's gossip chain seems to work even quicker than the Beauties'.

Ashely takes me to the library. There's a fire burning, and the handset of an old-timey landline sits off its cradle on a small, round wooden side table.

Ashely leads me to the cushy chair. "You okay? You let me know if you need anything. Anything at all."

I give her a nod as she leaves me. "Thanks, Ashely."

I wait till I hear the door close to say hello.

It's Shannon. She's sobbing into the phone. "Charlie. You have to come back, I need you."

"Shannon, what's happened?"

"It's M—Mark." She's crying so hard she can barely get the words out. "He died. On our honeymoon. A—a d—diving accident."

Ice creeps through my bloodstream, frozen fingers plucking at my spine. My mind drifts back to the dark place. An officer from the island putting a heavy hand on my shoulder. His words now echo in my mind.

Ma'am. I'm sorry. There's been an accident.

This can't be happening.

My heart chills to a block of ice, my stomach sinks to the floor. I think I'm going to be sick.

This can't be happening.

Not again.

CHAPTER NINETEEN

Charlie

I have to leave. I have to go to Shannon. All my other thoughts are a cloudy mess, flashes of my own nightmare honeymoon mixed with the replay of the pain in Shannon's voice on the phone. How did this happen? Why did it happen? And how can it not be related to my own husband's death?

Coincidences are events that happen without obvious connections, as if by accident, chance, or fate. Two Bachman men both dying in mysterious diving accidents at the Cayman Islands on their honeymoons?

This is not a coincidence.

I have to go to Shannon, but also, I need to speak with Rockland. I need to know what he knows and how this is connected to my past. I know he'll tell me as much as he can. I just hope it's enough to ease my mind.

Shannon's call not only dredged up all kinds of memories, but also the fact that I'm cursed with men and should continue to keep them all at arm's length. I have to go to Nikolaos and tell him the truth.

It's time for me to leave Dark Island.

I have to help my friend.

My gut sinks. It's time for me to leave…

Him.

We've been going back and forth for a full day. "Debating." He doesn't want me to go. I can tell by the tone of his voice, the steely set of his jaw, the Beast is sooo not happy with me returning to the Village.

We're standing on the dock at the boathouse, waiting for the boat. I'm bundled up, wearing a scarf and a heavy coat, winter fighting on her way out. He crosses his arms over his chest, making his biceps look absolutely massive. Like he needed to look any more intimidating than he already does. His booming voice rumbles through the room. "You know you aren't going unless you agree to my terms."

I give his arm a gentle touch and offer him a reassuring smile. "You don't have to talk so loud. It's just us."

"Sorry," he grumbles. "But I mean it."

"I know. Aiden will be right by my side. All the way to the Village. Then posted outside my front door until *you've* deemed it safe for him to return. I got it." I stressed the word *you've* because he's repeated this so many times to me now.

Nikolaos is the only one who will decide when I'm safe enough to lose my 24/7 bodyguard. I've had one before, after my botched choice in fiancés. A brother was with me for weeks but they're pretty good at blending into the background and letting you live your life.

As long as you do what they say.

"He's a good man. You're in good hands." He gives another one of those gruff grunting sounds he's known for. I don't even think he's aware he does it. "Not as good of hands as you'd be in if you'd just stay put, here at the castle with me, of course."

The grunting, his nickname and the mention of the castle makes me feel so much like Belle, I almost have to stifle a giggle. Then I remember I'm leaving him, and any amusement drains from me. I'm going home. To be alone. Again.

"Shannon needs me," I say for what feels like the hundredth time in the past 24 hours.

He grunts for the hundredth time in the past 24 hours.

The sun spreads out over the horizon, oranges and pinks and reds widening across the waterline, melting across the sky. The boat engine happily hums as the boat makes its way toward us.

My things at home had been in the process of being packed when I got the call. By the time I get there, everything will be back in place. All I have is the Vera Bradley bag I came with. Nikolaos is staying here. He won't be accompanying me on the trip.

He wraps his arms around me. "So this is goodbye?"

"Yes. It is." I lean up on tiptoe to plant a chaste kiss on his cheek.

He grabs my chin, tipping my lips to meet his. He kisses me deeply, leaving me breathless, my head cloudy. He kisses me again, making me want to beg him to make me stay. When he breaks away, his eyes stay glued to mine.

"Come back anytime. Come back all the time." The way he looks at me makes me feel like he wants to finish his statement with, *Come back, forever.*

"Okay. Thank you." I bend down, lifting my bag from the ground to put it over my shoulder.

He takes the bag from me, carrying it to the boat that will take me to the mainland. "Stay safe. Stay inside the walls of the Village till you get the all-clear from Aiden."

I don't want him to worry. "I will. I promise."

"I'd say call me to let me know when you get to the Village…"

"But you'll already know," I laugh, thinking of the tabs the drivers and security brothers keep on us Beauties.

I have to be the one to break away, to turn and leave. I don't look back. I can't. Aiden follows me like a comforting shadow, keeping me safe and offering me his hand as I step onto the boat. I can't help but wish it was Nikolaos escorting me.

We return to the Village. With Aiden planted outside, I enter my house. It's cold and dark. Hannah is a conservationist and cut off the heat and lights when she left. It's so quiet, the sound of me setting my soft cloth bag down on the wood floors sounds loud to me. I flick on a light.

There's a fresh bouquet of yellow roses, our symbol of friendship, waiting for me on my hall table. Other than the flowers, there's no sign anyone's been here. No pitter-patter of little feet to greet me, welcoming me home. No kiss from my man. No whisper that I've been missed brushing against my ear.

Nothing.

I go to the kitchen to Captain Jack Sparrow's tank, looking for some kind of greeting, however small.

"Hey, buddy. Did you miss me?" I tap on the glass, searching for him. He's not in his pirate ship. I don't see him anywhere. My gaze rises to the surface of the water where his beautiful blue and red body floats. "You have got to be kidding me."

Jack Sparrow has died too. I know beta fish only live two to five years and I've had him for five, but still. Tears are shed as I bury his little body in my back garden and clean out his tank.

Now, to find Shannon.

My already heavy heart sinks further, a cold weight like an anvil hollowing out my chest. I want to be there for her, to offer her support in her time of need. Who better than me knows how she suffers?

Selfishly, I already feel drained by my own life. Charlie, get over yourself. Your friend needs you. I buck up, walking down the street toward her gray townhouse.

She answers the door on the first knock, throwing it open and falling into my arms. "Oh, Charlie! You came."

The warmth of her hug fills me with guilt for my earlier selfish thoughts. I'm instantly glad I came. "I'd say I can't imagine what you're going through but…"

She looks at me with tear-filled eyes. "You're the one person on this earth who knows exactly how I feel."

"Exactly." I take her hand. "Come. I'll make you some tea."

"Thanks. Everyone's been here around the clock, but I sent them all home when I heard you'd gotten into town. I wanted a little time to decompress with you."

"That sounds like a good idea." My stomach flip-flops at the thought of having to relive the pain she's going through. I swallow it back, knowing my job is to be here for her, no matter what I'm feeling.

I miss Nikolaos…

I get her settled on her sofa, snuggling cozy blankets around her. "I'll be right back up with tea."

I put her kettle on to boil, flipping through tea bags. I choose chamomile for its calming properties. Shuffling through her cupboard I find a package of cookies and place a few on a plate. Neither of us feels like eating, but I want to get something in her stomach. I pick a few winter pansies from her back garden, separate the flowers from the stems, and organize the pretty purple and yellow blooms on a tray with teacups and the cookies.

My heart and my footsteps feel heavy as I make my way up the stairs to her living room.

She's dabbing at her eyes with the tissues I left her. "Thanks so much for coming. I hated to pull you away from whatever you were up to, but what happened to…" her lower lip trembles as she tries to get her late husband's name out, "M—Mark, happened to your husband too."

"I know. Did they say what happened?"

"I only know there was what the brothers call foul play." She shakes her head. Her eyes go stony and cold, her chilling tone sending shivers down my spine. "This was no accident."

"Oh." My head spins. At the time, I'd been told my husband had ascended too quickly from deep water. And that dissolved nitrogen formed bubbles in his blood. That he'd died of decompression sickness, or "the bends." "And you weren't with him on the scuba excursion?"

"No. It was the only thing I wanted to sit out on. We went snorkeling together, but I went shopping while he was scuba diving. I didn't care for all the equipment."

Someone wanted him alone, just like my late husband. My stomach turns as I think of what could have happened to the men. Were they drowned? Were they given faulty air tanks? My hands begin to shake. I feel queasy.

I'm not so sure I'm the best help for Shannon. I'm barely holding on right now. I feel so weak, and I just want to be in Nikolaos's arms.

I want to know more. I also don't want to think about this at all. It's so hard. "I don't know what to say. I need to talk to Rockland."

"You should." She gives a little laugh. "Maybe he can give you more information than he gave me. He told me basically nothing."

"To keep you safe." I put my hand gently over hers. "Rockland would only keep us in the dark if it was to protect us."

"I know." She takes a sip of her tea. "It's still hard."

I ask her about the rest of the trip, getting her to smile at the good parts, the happy memories they'd made together. "Hold on to those thoughts," I say. "When times get tough, you just keep thinking of those magical moments you had together."

I change the subject, asking her questions about Ireland, trying to keep the mood light. She talks of her family and how much she misses them. Tess texts me to tell me Shannon hasn't eaten much and to see if I can get some food into her. I spend twenty minutes naming every place I can think of that is allowed to deliver to the gates of the Village. Finally, we settle on soup from the French place on the corner.

Which only makes me think of Remy and his good cooking at the castle.

She has a bowl of soup and a roll. I put extra butter on the bread, trying to build in a few extra calories. After we eat, she's fading fast, the chamomile and grief taking hold of her. I take her up to her bed, tucking her in like a child. I offer to stay with her, but she says she'll be fine. She's planning on taking a melatonin tablet and passing out.

I stay till she falls asleep, pulling the covers all the way up to her chin.

Aiden walks me back home and the moment I close the door, my phone rings. It's Rockland. I'm sure Aiden informed him of my return.

Rockland is a powerful man. Tall with large muscles, dark, shorn hair, a cropped beard. He has the tattoo on his chest like the other brothers in Greece. Nikolaos has one too. It's super sexy. Rockland's a fearless leader, lethal and brilliant, but he hates attention on him. And he prefers to drive his old pickup truck, Thunder, over all the fancy sports cars he could afford.

He's an amazing leader. As caring as he is deadly. He'll be anxious to speak to me and fill me in as best he can.

I pick up the phone with shaky hands. "Rockland. How are you?"

"I've been better. You never get over the pain of losing a brother. How are you, Charlie?"

"I'm holding up. Mark's death has shaken the entire family, that's for sure."

"We're having the celebration of life in a few weeks."

"I'll be sure to be there."

"So, I'm guessing you've noticed the similarities between your late husband and Mark's deaths."

"Yes." Thinking of Shannon, I swallow back the tears. "Too similar to be a coincidence."

"Correct. I'm sorry we couldn't tell you there was foul play when your husband was killed." Hearing him say that word, *killed,* strikes my heart. Before now, we'd always said "died." He died. Now, the past has changed.

"We thought the less you knew, the better," Rockland says.

"It's okay. I understand." I think of the women in the boathouse. "I know some secrets are kept in order to keep people safe. What can you tell me?"

"I assume you know by now what we are doing on Dark Island."

"Yes."

"Right," he says. "We'll leave that at that. But you need to know, the two deaths are definitely linked. Your husband was working on the same ring. It was just budding at the time, and we tried to put a stop to it. Your husband was a casualty of that attempt. We realized at the time we weren't strong enough, that we weren't ready to tackle such a thing. We didn't want to lose another brother."

My husband was the first one to try to attempt this feat? I had no idea. "I thought he was in finances for the family?"

"He started there. Then, it was a great cover as we branched out to try this. I'm really sorry we lost him, Charlie."

How do I say I'm over him? Such a brave man? He deserved more admiration than I gave him. I don't know what to say. I just wait for Rockland to speak again.

"You doing okay, Charlie?"

"Yes, sir. I'm fine."

"And Shannon? You girls are taking good care of her?"

"Yes, sir. We are."

"Charlie," Rockland says. "I want to say I'm sorry. I know this is hard."

"Thanks. I appreciate that."

We say our goodbyes.

My husband died. Now, Mark has died. Nikolaos could die too. The stakes are high enough with his job. His operation is dangerous enough without me plaguing him with the Charlie curse.

Okay...*logically,* intellectually, I realize there's no curse. But emotionally, given all I've experienced in my life, I can't shake the thought. I'm still convinced it's there, because regardless of the cause, stuff keeps happening to me.

My spiral of thinking leads me to one, sad conclusion: I can't be with him.

It wouldn't be fair to him.

I don't want to put him at risk.

And the full truth? The real reason, the one that keeps me up at night...

After all the heartache in my life...

If I lost him...

I don't think I could survive the pain.

CHAPTER TWENTY

Beast Shannon had been eager to jet out of the Village the day of their wedding. Mark told his wife he wanted a few weeks to hang out at the townhouse, settle into married life, but really he wanted to help run the last shipment of girls. He took care of the city end of things, getting the girls from their hovel onto the boat.

I make it a habit not to drink hard liquor. Enough foolish men who couldn't control themselves, even before they were inebriated, flowed through my mother's life that I stayed away from the stuff.

Tonight, I pour myself a whiskey, neat.

Mark was my partner in the destruction of crime. Well, this particular crime, this human trafficking ring. We both broke enough laws to serve more than a few life sentences. That's just the way it is when you're a Bachman. Some rules are meant to be broken.

Mark's death confirms what we were starting to suspect. The leader of the ring is onto us. He knows exactly who's causing him to bleed girls, and he knew Mark was the one getting them out. Let's just hope he doesn't know where they were going. We've had to put a pause on taking any more shipments to the island right now. It's just too dangerous for them.

God damn, I'm going to miss Mark.

I sip my whiskey, thinking of his good sense of humor that even got a laugh out of me from time to time. Shannon is devastated. I'm glad Charlie has gone to be by her side but having her out from under my wing of protection has my gut wrenching.

I pour a second whiskey. This one's to drown my sorrow over missing Charlie. She was only on Dark Island for a matter of days, but she made such a permanent impression on my life. The castle feels empty without her beautiful, smiling face.

A glance down at my watch tells me I've only been without her for five hours. When they asked what I wanted for dinner, I told them I wouldn't be eating. I'm like a damn child, sulking in her absence.

The whiskey goes straight to my head. I pick up my phone and dial her number. She answers on the second ring.

"Hello?"

The sound of her voice alone is enough to make me hard.

"Hey. How's Shannon?"

Charlie spends ten minutes updating me. The entire time she's speaking all I can think is… when is she coming back? But the longer she talks, the more I begin to sense she's not.

"You're not coming back here. Are you?" I try to keep the petulant, grumpy, childish tone from my voice. I twirl my glass between my finger and thumb, staring at the light bouncing off the amber liquor while I wait for her to answer.

She gives a little sigh. "No. I'm not."

"Just because of Shannon?" I ask.

But I already know the answer, don't I? A woman doesn't turn you down multiple times over multiple occasions, then magically want you after spending a few days with you. She wouldn't disrupt her life like that.

"N—no. I'm sorry. I just think it would be best if we…"

If she says the *f* word, I'm going to throw up.

She takes another shaky breath. "If we just go back to being friends."

I'm going to throw up. "No," I say. "I don't want that. I want you."

"I know. And I'm sorry. I just think this is best."

"What are you wearing?" I ask, not wanting to let the conversation end but no longer able to handle the direction it's going.

She gives a little giggle. "Seriously?"

"Seriously." I throw back a quarter of my whiskey. "When have you ever known me to not be serious?"

"I find you quite playful at times. Playful and—"

"Don't say it. Do. Not. Say it."

"Sweet!" She gives another giggle.

"What happened to you the last time you called me sweet?"

"You spanked me and put a vibrating plug in my ass?" she says.

I give a gruff chuckle at her matter-of-fact answer. A few days ago she could barely say "cock." "And you loved it."

"I did."

"I know," I say. "I want to do it again. Right now."

"Too bad we're miles and miles apart."

Hmm... I have a thought. "I'll bet you have a vibrator there at your house, though, don't you?"

"Maaaaybe..."

"I bet you're going to do exactly what I say and go get that vibrator right now."

"You know what they say about making bets?" she giggles.

I rack my brain for sayings about bets. Can't think of any. "No. What do they say?" The thought of her using her vibrator on herself makes me sit back further in my chair, spreading my legs wide. I slip my hand down my jeans and rub my cock.

She pauses, then laughs, her pretty voice getting me harder. "I don't know. Is there a saying about making bets?"

"Not that I'm aware of." I rub harder to ease the ache in my cock. "Now go and get that vibrator."

She gives what sounds like an exasperated sigh, but I hear the sound of a drawer opening. It sounds like she's getting comfortable somewhere. "Okay," she says. "I have it."

God, this is such a turn on. My cock grows harder in my hand. "What kind is it?"

"One of those little kidney bean-shaped ones."

"So you like it on your clit?" I ask.

"Yes."

"Turn it on. Let me hear it."

There's a click and a soft buzzing sound. Knowing she's there, doing what I say, it's such a fucking turn on.

"Slide it down your pants. Hold it on your clit."

"Mmm..."

"You like that, baby?" I ask. "Does that feel good?"

"Mmm hmm..."

"Do you wish it was my mouth on you, licking your sweet pussy and pleasuring you?"

"Yes, I do."

I bark the command, "Turn it off."

"Wh—what?"

"You heard me."

She gives a little whimper as she cuts it off.

"Tell me what you'd want me to do to you if I was there with you right now."

"Hmm... I'd want you to fuck me."

"How would you want me to fuck you?"

"From the back. Hands and knees."

"Good girl. Turn it back on." I picture us on my stairs that morning, the naughty look of surprise on her face when I caught her. I imagine taking her from the back.

"Uhh...mmm...I'm getting close."

I jack off faster, my balls tightening as I get closer to orgasm. "Me too."

She makes that sexy little mewing sound as she comes. "Yes, mmm, yes."

"Baby. Baby." I hold my dick as I climax. Cum runs over my hand, hot and wet. "God damn that feels good."

"Yeah." Her voice sounds dreamlike. "I needed that."

"Next time it'll be my cock making you moan."

She clears her throat. "Nikolaos. There won't be a next time. We need to say goodbye."

"I'll say goodbye. For now."

"Goodbye. You have to forget about me." And she hangs up.

I feel that burning in my chest. Yearning for her. Wanting her.

Her words only make me do the opposite. They fuel me to jump into planning mode. I have to get her back here with me. The Village is walled in with gates and both human and technical surveillance, but I'd be giving her 24-7 protection, never taking my eyes off of her. No one else can offer her that.

And I don't want to spend another night in this damn castle without her.

She has to come back here.

I have to bring her back.

I think...

I think...

God.

Damn.

I think I'm in love with her.

How can I be throwing that word around so casually? It isn't love. It can't be. It was only a few days. Sure, they were the best days of my life, but you can't know—you can't claim to feel something *that* strong, say *that* word, after a matter of days.

Can you?

I clean myself up, needing a walk in the cool night air to clear my mind and to plan. I'm walking along the shore. There's a light on the water near our dock. A circular white light. Possibly an approaching boat?

My hackles rise. Could be nothing. In our world? It's always something.

I'm out here alone. We have security planted on different parts of the island, guards constantly on watch. Surely someone else saw the light as well. Should I turn back and raise the alarm? Investigate on my own?

I'm deciding when I hear a whizzing sound fly through the air. There's a thunk. A burning in my chest. Pain. Blinding pain. White light. Humming noise vibrating through my eardrums. My hand goes to my chest, my fingers pulling away with something dark and warm and wet covering them.

Have I been shot?

I fall to the ground.

There're footsteps coming close, boots crunching over the sticks on the ground. A face hovers over me. Familiar but distant. It's him. The shifty punk that arranged the last shipment. The one that favors fake leather. He brings a radio to his mouth. "Not yet but soon. He's close."

I knew there was something off about that kid. Should have trusted my gut.

There're shouts in the woods. The familiar voices of my men. The kid takes off.

I lie there, staring up at the moon, not knowing whether I'm living or dying. The air is so crisp, the sky, so beautiful. Is this heaven? The first time I came to this island and saw the castle, I knew this place was as close as I'd ever get. I almost laugh. There's no way in hell I'll be making it into heaven. Good thing I don't believe in that kind of thing.

Voices call to me. Fingers and hands touching my chest, my neck. Faces float in front of me. They're the faces of my men but they're soon replaced by the angelic vision of Charlie's perfect image.

"Charlie."

One thing I know: if I am alive, being here with me is the last place I want Charlie. It's not safe for her here. I'm not safe for her. I couldn't protect myself. I didn't see this coming.

How could I possibly protect her?

If I live, I'll do exactly what she told me to.

Forget about her.

CHAPTER
TWENTY-ONE

Charlie

My slippered feet pad against the wood floors as I make my way to the front door. I've not bothered to change out of my PJs today; instead, I just tied a big, fluffy pink robe over them. I did brush my teeth and throw my hair in a cute messy bun this morning at least.

I open the door, holding the Lush box out to Aiden. "White or dark?"

He stares straight ahead, his hands folding in front of him. "You know I'm not supposed to take my eyes off the perimeter for a single second, ma'am."

On the long ride home, Aiden and I discovered that we had something in common. We're both chocolate lovers. "White or dark?"

He gives a pretend sigh. "If you're going to make me break protocol, I guess... white. The one with the almond paste in it, please?"

"Sure thing." I scan the box, finding two of the ones he wants. "Here you go. I'll be back with your coffee in an hour." He likes a four o'clock espresso. It keeps him focused till his night replacement comes so he can catch a few hours of sleep.

He breaks character for a moment, shooting me a beaming grin. "Thanks, Charlie."

I pad my way back to my sofa, sinking into the little nest I've created since I've been back. I bite into an oval-shaped dark chocolate. The inside is filled with crunchy coconut. I gag.

See? I knew I was cursed.

I spit it out into a clean tissue and toss it in the small trash can under the end table.

Smoothing my blanket over my lap—castle-side down because I can't bear to look at it right now—I pick up the remote, flipping through my options. I choose a cheesy rom-com I've seen at least three times.

She wants to love him, but scars from her loveless childhood are holding her back. Sound familiar? Spoiler alert, she gets over her fears, her hurts, and gets the guy. They live happily ever after in a little teal and yellow craftsman-style bungalow in Seattle, drinking coffees at the table outside the café where they first met when he spilled an espresso on her white sweater during the meet-cute, joined by their adorable goldendoodle.

I pop another chocolate in my mouth. This time, I triple checked the map on the lid of the package to be sure it's a good one. Mmm… caramel. My favorite.

The simple taste of the buttery caramel literally tears my heart in two. Cue the tears. Grab the tissues. It's the very same treat I ate at his castle. It reminds me of his sweet gesture, of how he added them onto my order as a surprise. I brought them with me. They're the chocolates I'm eating right now. When I ate that caramel chocolate in my bedroom in the castle, I remember how I was thinking of how happy I was to not be alone.

Buried under blankets and tissues.

Crying on my couch.

Much like I am now...

I think of how happy I was.

A wail bursts forth from me, echoing through my empty townhouse. The sound just makes me feel more self-hatred for the pathetic state I've put myself in. I'm right back where I was the night he chased me down at the club.

All the magic is drained from my life.

I'm back to Charlie the flower wearing, casserole baking, party planner... of other people's parties.

Geez, they're not even my own celebrations, are they? I couldn't tell you the last time I celebrated something. My cursed wedding?

Another wail creeps up and I try to hold it back but then the movie gets to the part where he accidentally hits her dog with his car and he's carrying the poor pup's limp body, running across the street to a vet, and she's standing on the street, crying, not sure if the dog is going to make it and I freaking lose it.

Shannon went home to be with her mom and sisters for a while. The few hours I was consoling her, she kept talking about her family back home. I thought it would be best if she was surrounded by them. I got Rockland to organize the jet for her and helped her pack. The Beauties don't need me like the girls at the castle did. They have their men, their lives. Their children.

Their goldendoodles…

I don't even have a fish.

Jack Sparrow died even though Hannah, a freaking scientist, was taking good care of him. He didn't stand a chance, belonging to me. He was cursed. Just like the rest of them.

I'm totally, utterly, alone. Just like I was my entire childhood, almost my entire adulthood. The curse following me around like a cloud, keeping me from having anyone in my life to love with my whole heart. No man, no baby.

He hasn't even called…

I know, I know. I told him to forget me. I wanted to protect him from my curse. But as the days went by, I couldn't help but to sit near the phone. Check that it was charged. Double-checked to be sure my ringer was on. He didn't call. He hasn't pursued me.

I finger the beautiful little flower encased in glass that hangs from the chain around my neck. White petals surround its cheery yellow core. It reminds me of the sun. I've not yet taken it off since he clasped it around my neck, only for showers to protect it from the water, but as soon as my skin is dry, it goes right back on.

I thought about changing my mind. Calling him. Telling him I was wrong, and my little pink vibrator misses his sexy voice.

But I can't. I've never, ever been able to be the pursuer. I know when I'm not wanted. I had an entire childhood of experience with it. I've never been one to burden someone with my presence. I didn't beg my own mother to want me.

Why would I bother a man I barely know?

She-devil says, *Because you're sitting here on your lonely ass which is expanding by the moment from the pounds of chocolate you're inhaling, and it's your fault because you told your soulmate to leave you alone.*

Would it be so weird? To call him? To tell him I've made a mistake?

Because right now, being without him is more painful than losing the other two combined.

I shoot him a text. Two little words that sum up my pain.

Missing you

My phone rings, instantly.

My heart lifts in my chest, a smile spreading across my face. I feel giddy, like a little kid getting a present. "It's him!"

I clear the chocolate and tears from my throat. "Hello?"

"Charlie, it's Ashely. Calling from Nikolaos's phone."

That's strange. Why would she be answering his phone? My mind instantly goes to my past. "Is he okay?"

Her professional tone is clipped, as if she's trying to contain her emotions. "Charlie, you should sit down. I need to tell you something."

"Ashely?" My fingers tighten around the phone. "What is it?"

"It's Nikolaos. He's hurt."

My heart sinks. My voice rises in pitch with each word. "What? When? What happened?"

"Last night. We didn't know if he was going to make it through the night, but thanks to his stubborn will and Dr. Williams, he's pulling through." She talks fast. I catch the words island, gunman, shot. This can't be true. What she's saying... it's not true. My head spins trying to process what she's telling me.

I stayed away. I tried to stay away to keep him safe. And still, the curse reached him? I never should have danced with him at that wedding. Gone down to that alley. Got in his car and rode to that island…

Ashely is still talking, but the words land like cotton balls, thick and soft, their lines blurred.

Then she says something that rings clear as a bell in my mind.

"The last thing he said…" Her voice breaks. "Was your name."

CHAPTER
TWENTY-TWO

Beast

The aqua waters of the Aegean Sea lap at my feet as I stroll the shore. I'm an Air Marshal for the Greek military. Dante has just started to recruit me. He's brought me to the Parrish. I'm alone, walking on the beach, thinking over the choice he laid in front of me.

To join the Bachmans.

The sun shines on me, warming my skin. This place feels like what heaven must be like. Did I make it to heaven? Am I still alive? A vague memory of Dr. Williams bustling around me, barking out orders to me to get better... a flash of Ashely's blonde hair as she reaches down to feel my forehead... Remy slipping sips of broth into my mouth, speaking to me in low tones, French words I don't understand.

And her...

She's here, in all of my memories. The first moment I saw her, standing there in that flower dress, the brother next to me saying, "That's Charlie, the widow." She's so beautiful, with a sadness behind that smile. I remember thinking, we're both surrounded by people we love. And she's just as lonely as I am.

I feel like she's here, somewhere nearby. I want to reach out, to grab her, pull her into me.

Ashely's voice breaks into my thoughts. "He has periods where he's more lucid. When he comes to, I'll tell him you came to visit. I know it will mean a lot to him."

"Thank you."

Charlie? She is here? I knew I could feel her. My heartbeat increases at the sound of her voice. Is she really here, or am I dreaming?

"I'm sorry." Her voice breaks. "I can't stay...it doesn't feel like my place."

"Don't worry. Dr. Williams only leaves his side for meals and sleep. And his staff is like family. We're in here chatting with him 'round the clock. Keeping him company. And the brothers from the Village have been great about visits. We've even had a few come all the way from the Parrish. Bronson and Paige will be here later today."

"So he has plenty of people caring for him? He's really going to be okay?"

Stay. Stay. Stay.

I feel like I'm screaming the word with all my strength and voice but I'm not because she doesn't respond to me.

She tells Ashely, "Good. That's good. I don't need to be here. I'll only put him further in danger."

"What do you mean?" Ashely asks.

The curse. The stupid, fucking curse. Don't go, Charlie.

Silence, and then Ashely says, "Never mind. I can see you don't want to talk about it. I'll walk you out."

No.

Stay. Stay. STAY.

The turquoise water laps at my feet. I run down the shore, sand kicking out behind my feet. I race down the beach, trying to find her. To stop her. To keep her here with me. The sun glints off the ripples at the top of the water, blinding me, making it difficult to see.

I can't find her.

She's gone.

CHAPTER
TWENTY-THREE

Charlie

I know he's not going to be here today. Ashely already called me and told me. She's good like that, knowing what's on a person's mind even when they don't share it with her. She knew I'd be looking for him here today, and likely she wanted to save me the pain.

He's fully healed, completed his marathon on the road to recovery. But he's not coming. Something with work keeping him on the island. In the back of my mind, I'm wondering if he's not coming because of me...

That he doesn't want to see me.

The thought breaks my heart.

Is it crazy that I'm still scanning the crowd for him, even when I know he's not here? My heart sinks to the soles of my white peep toe Louboutins. I want him. Even when I know I've made my decision and the man isn't even in the same darn zip code as me, I never, ever stop wanting him.

We stand in a beautiful meadow in the back of the Village. The grass here is green year-round, a mystery that has never been solved. Everyone wears white as it's a celebration of life, not death. When a member of the Brotherhood passes, all of the men spend the night before the ceremony in a closed chamber with the body of the deceased, as they did last night with Mark.

There's the sound of three claps. That's our signal to drop to our knees. Join hands with those beside us, heads bowed. Together, our voices rise as we chant, "Love lives on. Love lives on. Love lives on."

Rising from the earth in the center of the circle of family is a huge stone monument. Gray, brown and as old as the Bachmans. It continues to rise till it's over ten feet tall. A stone is removed from the monument.

Now it's the part of the ceremony where I'm going to lose it. The wife of a deceased Brother has to remove the necklace given to her by her husband on her wedding day and place it on the box of her husband's remains. Shannon does so, the box is placed behind the missing stone and the stone is replaced. The monument will lower back into the ground when the ceremony is over.

I can't watch, my own memories and pain still a burden. I never, ever want to be up there again, all eyes on me as I place my necklace on my husband's remains. Tess helps her and I stay kneeling, my eyes shut tightly.

My breaths start to come too fast, my heart thumping in my chest too hard. Blood whooshes in my ears and I feel faint. It's too much, this whole thing, it's like reliving my husband's death, losing the baby, leaving Beast.

I gently ease myself out of the circle, excusing myself as I tiptoe across the meadow. When I'm a respectful distance away, I break out into a run. I have to get away from this rock, the body. Tears start to flow, blurring my vision. My breaths are still coming fast. I'm on the verge of hyperventilating.

My hand goes to my queasy belly. My vision starts to go fuzzy, black circles closing in as I grow more faint. I need to find somewhere to sit before I collapse.

Strong hands grab my shoulders. "You couldn't handle the crowd either?"

He's…here? I'd heard he wasn't able to make it. I told my heart and my little she-devil to count him out so we can continue to move on with our lonely lives.

"You're here." I look up and our eyes meet. And in this moment, I can no longer deny the truth. I am selfish. I would risk him being taken by my curse. I need him that badly.

"You okay?" His familiar voice. It instantly calms me, the stress draining from my body.

He can clearly see that I'm not. Instead of waiting for an answer, he just folds me into his arms. And I just cry. My cheek presses against the soft fabric of his white shirt; it'll be ruined with my tears in a matter of moments. I don't care and the loving way he rubs my back tells me he doesn't care either.

He leans down, his words ruffling the curls at the top of my head. "God, I've missed you."

"I—I've m—missed you too," I choke out between sobs. "Every minute."

My confession makes him give a little chuckle. "Good. I'm glad to hear I'm not the only who was going crazy being apart."

"Yeah, I was starting to feel really..." Desperate? Defeated? Like life was no longer worth living? I can't find a word that adequately describes the pain I carried around in my chest. Finally, I put my finger on it. "Brokenhearted."

He wraps his arms tighter around me, his protective warmth enveloping me. He rests his chin on the top of my head. His words are soft. "You know there's a simple solution to all that pain."

"I know," I say.

"But I guess being here at" —his voice breaks as he says his friend's name— "Mark's celebration of life, it's bringing up too many memories for you to change your mind, isn't it?"

"Yes. No." I shake my head. "I don't know. All I know is that I want to be with you. And I don't want to get hurt."

He cups my face in his hands, making me look up at him. "But you're hurting now."

"I know."

"What if the decision was taken away from you?"

"What do you mean?"

"I'm no longer letting you choose." He drops my face, bends down, slips his strong arms behind my back and under the backs of my legs, and scoops me up in the air like a bride going over the threshold. "I'm kidnapping you. Again."

"Right now? Here?" A giggle escapes me as he tightens his hold on me, my feet dangling in the air.

"Yes. Right here, right now." He turns on a bootheel, carrying me as if my weight is nothing to him. He heads away from the meadow. "I said my private goodbyes to Mark this morning. The sun was rising. I could feel his presence. I wanted to let you have the opportunity to go to his ceremony, but it looks like you're ready to go sooner than I thought."

It's symbolic as we walk away from the meadow, him carrying me away from death. I'm going to leave the curse behind me in that rock. At the end of the ceremony, it will go back down in the ground where it came from and be buried, and I'll be free.

Bad things might happen. Well, it's life, so bad things are sure to come. But I'm not willing to live my life without him, in fear that one day I might lose him.

I'm going to decide that the curse is broken. Living my life thinking there's a dark cloud over me that puts every man I love in danger is no way to live. I stare up at his handsome face, and I let the idea of the curse waft away like a puff of smoke.

My little she-devil reminds me of what used to be my favorite Walt Whitman quote, when I was younger and filled with hope. *Remember this one,* she says. *'Tis better to have loved and lost, than never to have loved at all.* I'm proud of her, finally thinking with something other than her libido.

I'm going to live by that quote, maybe even cross-stitch it for my wall.

My little she-devil breaks away from her sentimental moment. *Who are you kidding? You're going to be too busy sexing your man to be doing any damn cross-stitching.*

"You are so very right." I lean up, stealing a kiss from Nikolaos.

He accepts the kiss, then gives me a curious look. "So very right that you're ready to go?"

Oops... I was talking out loud to my little she-devil. I flick my hand along my shoulder, sending her flying. I let her go.

Forever.

"So," I say, changing subjects to cover up the fact I was actually talking to myself, "where are we headed?"

The smile that breaks out over his face is one I'll keep with me for the rest of my life. He leans down, planting a sweet kiss on my forehead. "To the most beautiful place in the world. First, we need to go to your place to pack."

It's strange, having him here at my place. He's never been here before. I take him up to the living room.

He spies the blanket he gives as takeaway gifts to visitors. It's folded neatly over the back of my sofa, showing off the photo of the castle. "You kept the blanket."

"And the chocolates." I lift one of the half-eaten boxes from the sofa side table. "Want one?"

"I'm good. Got all the sugar I need." He leans down to kiss me. The kiss starts slowly but grows into something more passionate, reminding me we're here alone. He kisses my earlobe, tickling my skin with his words. "I want to see the vibrator. The one you used on yourself that night I called you on the phone."

"You do, do you?" He doesn't give me any room for privacy as far as sex goes, does he? I lean into his kiss, loving the warm, tickling feel of his lips against my skin. "Then you'll have to come up to the bedroom."

I feel shy, taking his hand and leading him up to my bedroom. One I've never shared with a man. It's strange being here with him, but exciting too. Part of me just wants him to scoop me up and take me to his castle. The other part knows that we're going to be spending the night here at my townhouse together, so I should enjoy it.

Hopefully, this will be my little farewell party to the townhouse. I'm ready to move on with my life.

It's time for Charlie 2.0 to start her new life. And my first challenge? Opening that nightstand drawer and handing him the little pink vibrator, not knowing what he'll do with it. My palms feel a little sweaty as I go to the nightstand.

It sits in the drawer, looking innocent enough, but I know when he gets his hands on something, he can turn it into a pleasure-torture device. I take a deep breath, and no longer needing my she-devil's encouragement, I pick it up on my own.

He stands in my bedroom, looking massive and masculine beside the antique frame of my queen-sized bed. He has that sexy smile on his handsome face. He holds out his hand to me.

I stare at his empty palm.

"Come on. Gimme." He beckons with a curl of his fingers.

I put the vibrator in his hand, my heart racing as I seal my fate.

He turns it over in his fingers. "Nice. It's cute."

"It was fun, that night on the phone," I say, still feeling shy.

"I have something to tell you about that night."

The way his eyes lock on mine makes my stomach drop. What could he have to tell me? "Just say it."

He glances down at the little toy, flipping it over in his hand. "That night after I got off the phone with you, I knew I was in love with you. I decided I was going to come and get you. But my plans got delayed."

"Oh my gosh, was that the night you got hurt?"

"Yeah. It was. I was lying there in the dark, not knowing if I was living or dying, and it changed my mind. I decided you were safer without me. If I couldn't protect myself, how could I protect you?"

"I had fears about hurting you too. I'm glad we got over them and we're together now. That's what matters."

"I love you, Charlie." He leans down, kissing my forehead.

Happiness flows through me, hearing him say those words. "I love you too." I never thought I'd hear those words from someone again, much less say them and get this warm feeling all over my body when I do.

"I love you, and now, I want to play with you." He turns the vibrator on, the soft buzzing sound filling the room. And I'm in his arms. And he's kissing me. And I'm melting against him.

He's slipping his hand down between our bodies, hitching up the skirt of my dress. He rubs the vibrator over my panties, lightly, his touch barely there. My panties are made of silk and the plastic vibrator slips over them. I give a little shiver as it hums against me.

He nips at my earlobe. "I see someone's finally wearing panties tonight."

"I thought it was appropriate for the occasion." Can't think. My head lolls back as the toy works its magic. He rubs it lightly up and down my sex. "Can't go panty-less to a memorial service."

His kisses travel down my neck, sucking and biting, making me moan. He turns off the toy, tossing it on the bed. "And now I get the pleasure of taking them off."

His mouth finds mine, kissing me hard. His tongue swipes against mine, hot and possessive. I fall into his kiss, spiraling down a tunnel of heat and desire. Now that we've said those words, the kiss is deeper, our lips somehow connecting our souls.

His hands are exploring underneath my dress, grabbing the waistband of my panties. He tugs them down. I step out of them. He slides the silky white panties into the pocket of his trousers. "A little keepsake for me."

He grabs the hem of my dress, lifting it up. Slowly, I raise my arms, Charlie 2.0 holding his gaze in what I hope is a sexy way. It must work because it earns me a powerful growl as he tugs the dress up and over my head.

To discover... I wear no bra.

His eyes go wide at the surprise sight of my bare breasts, my nipples tightening from excitement. "No bra?"

"It would have ruined the dress," I say.

"Come here. My God, you're gorgeous, aren't you?" His hands travel down my slowly lowering arms, cupping my ribcage, smoothing down my sides, encircling my waist.

"You're pretty easy on the eyes yourself. Let's get you undressed." I help him out of his shirt. I trace the outline of the tattoo on his chest with my fingertip—something I've wanted to do for a long time. "I love this."

"And I love you." He lays me down on the bed, kissing every inch of my body. When he enters me, he keeps his eyes on mine, one hand cupping the side of my face. He kisses me and tells me he loves me. Our bodies move together like they were made for each other. When we come, we come together, our lips locked in a deep kiss, our arms wrapped around one another in an embrace so tight, so safe, so full of satisfaction, it makes me whole.

Twenty-four hours later, we're standing hand in hand on the shore of the Parrish. A gentle breeze flutters the hem of my aqua dress — it's the same one I wore that night in the alleyway, a special request by him. Thank goodness for Mr. Allen, my tailor in the city who was able to repair the dirty knee scuffs on it. Nikolaos wears the suit he wore at our boat dinner at my request, as that's the night we've since declared our first official date.

The sun warms our skin. What is it about the sun that feels so healing? I close my eyes and turn my face up to the sky, welcoming the wonderful energy.

I lean against him, snuggling against his big, strong arm. "This really is beautiful."

"Correction. The most beautiful place on earth." He slips something from his pocket. "I have something for you."

It's a gold ring. He holds it out to me, letting me see it. It's beautiful, a wide gold band. A bright diamond sits in the center, ovals surrounding the center like rays, the raised design crisscrossing and growing larger as they burst out from the gem.

"It's the sun. Because you're my sun. Every time you enter a room, every time I lay eyes on your beautiful face, you warm me like I'm standing here, at my favorite place on earth. You warm me like the sun shining on me. And the sun gives life. You, Charlie Bachman, give me life."

And he drops to one knee.

"Oh my gosh…"

He looks up at me, holding the ring up to me. "Charlie Bachman, will you marry me?"

I've left the curse behind. But he can still see the worry in my eyes.

That big, bright smile that's become my personal sun spreads over his handsome face. "I'll take my chances," he says.

"Then, yes." I hold out my left hand, letting him slip the ring on my finger. "I'd love to."

He stands, leaning down and kissing me so deeply, I feel tingles all the way down to my toes.

"Do you like the ring?"

"I love the ring. It's unique and beautiful and every time I look at it, I'll remember your sweet words." He cringes at the word "sweet." "And you're going to learn, as my husband, I'll call you sweet all I want."

He looks down at the ring. "The band is a little wider than the rings you normally wear but there's a reason for that."

I love the thickness and width of the band. It's solid, like our connection. "Why?"

"So if there ever is a time when I'm not with you—which I don't plan on happening often—I want every man around you to be able to see it and know you are mine."

I give a soft laugh at that. It's sweet, but ridiculous. "Nikolaos, you need to know—you're the only man I've laid eyes on in almost a decade. When I first saw you at the Benefit Ball at the Hamlet, I couldn't take my eyes off of you."

"Still. I'm happier with it on you. They need to know you're taken."

I like how he thinks men would be checking me out. It's flattering. I give off such a Betty Homemaker vibe. I'm rarely hit on. Maybe Charlie 2.0 would get some looks in her sexy little black dresses, but it wouldn't matter anyway.

He's the only man for me.

We spend the week swimming in the sea, warming ourselves in the sun, dining with family. At the end of the week, he takes my hand in his and says, "Let's go home." And I know by home, he means back to his castle because he knows there's no place I'd rather be.

This Beauty finally has her Beast.

CHAPTER TWENTY-FOUR

Beast

Now that I'm going to have a wife living here, the boathouse will no longer be a safehouse. I won't risk Charlie's safety. Dark Island is going back to being just my home. A tucked away place for Charlie and any children we might have one day.

I'm trying my darnedest to get one in her belly, taking the opportunity to try to impregnate her every chance I get. So far, she's not made a single complaint. In fact, every night she's shouting, "More! Please. More!"

I'm no longer helping with the dismantling of the trafficking ring since my name being out there with the ringleaders has taken me out of the loop. Instead, I'm working with the family in a new capacity. We're going to continue to use the lake for shipping. We've decided we'll be investing in gold, and we'll be storing it on the island. I'm in the process of building a secure warehouse on the far north end of the property.

Charlie immediately dived into a project, converting the now-empty boathouse into a B&B for the family. Anyone who needs a weekend escape can travel to Dark Island for a day or two, do some boating, have a meal on the riverboat in the boathouse, have a drink in the speakeasy.

Bronson and Paige have already booked it for their tenth wedding anniversary.

Charlie's completely redecorated the place. She kept the dining room she redid the first time she was here, since that was already done to her standards, but everything else has changed. She's created three guest rooms. All done up in flower themes.

She has her Botanical Boho Room, filled with earthy tones, wallpaper with green-leafed plants, tons of lush green potted plants and shelves of small ceramic pots filled with succulents. Then there's her favorite, the Begonia Room. There's a mural of huge, colorful flowers painted on the walls and soft quilted bedding on the gold-framed bed. And the Lilac Room, a pale purple room filled with vases of dried lavender, gold-framed prints of lilacs hanging on the walls.

Charlie wants it to be a throwback in time, a place to relax and get away from the busyness of the city. She added a small kitchen that's fully stocked for whenever a visitor might not want to be disturbed by staff. The main room where we used to have the beds is now a living room with deep-cushioned gray velour sofas. She has a record player with hundreds of vinyl records stashed away in the record cabinet, and a television with no internet but a DVD player and a cabinet of all kinds of old movies to choose from. She says there's nostalgia in having low tech and also opted for sets of cards and shelves of books and board games.

Leaning against the outside wall of the boathouse she's got a few lightweight canoes. There's a shed she added as well as paddleboards, and life vests organized perfectly. I had to put my foot down when she wanted to paint the sides of the boathouse, so she had the shed's siding painted in a floral mural similar to the one in the Begonia Room.

She even brought in a hot tub, something she used to dream about when she was a little girl. Apparently, a friend of hers had one when she was growing up and they just looked so fun to her, she wanted one out here. She housed it in a little gazebo, the roof of the gazebo clear glass so you can see the stars at night when you're soaking in the hot tub.

Owning a bicycle was another little girl dream of hers. Beach bikes with wide tires are parked at a covered bike rack, next to higher-tech mountain bikes for use on the gravel paths that wind through the woods. She even bought a bike trailer for parents to tug their little ones behind them on a ride.

Charlie continues her work for the women. She hates that she has to do it from a distance, that she can't hold their hands and give them manicures, but she does what she can, keeping our safehouses stocked with clothing and shoes. Each new safehouse we open I take her to decorate and put her homey touches on things, but forty-eight hours before any shipment arrives, we're back, safe at home.

I may be the boss in the bedroom, but what Charlie says at the castle goes. She's the head of the household now, running the castle and our staff the way she wants it done. Which, in classic Charlie fashion, is absolutely perfect. The staff are smitten with her, even more than they were when she first arrived, and they've welcomed her with open arms. Her feminine touch softens my hard edges.

They like that. A lot.

No matter how busy our individual days are, Charlie and I know every night we're going to be sitting down to dinner together. Tonight we're having her favorite: Chef Remy's take on pasta carbonara.

After dinner, we have a glass of wine in the speakeasy. My segue into an invitation to my dungeon. She, of course, accepts.

I feel that tugging in my chest, only now I know I can act on it freely. It's a longing for the woman who will soon be my wife. I just want to be close to her, inside of her, feel her naked body against mine.

We undress one another slowly. I sit down on that same black leather chair, pulling her down on my lap, facing me, just like I did the first time I brought her down to my dungeon. I guide her pussy onto my cock and suck in a breath of air as she forms around me, the feeling so fucking good I can barely function.

"I can't believe we said I love you before I ever got to touch your tattoo." She strokes her fingers over the swirling black pattern covering my left pectoral muscle as she rides me.

I lift my hips, burying myself in her. "I've seen you eyeing it."

"Every single night. It's pretty sexy." She strokes my face. "And this beard. I love this beard."

I run my fingers over my facial hair. "Yeah, I shaved it for that first date, but I let it grow back."

"I love it. Keep it forever." She gives a little giggle as she rolls her hips, finding her rhythm. "It makes you my furry beast."

"Your sweet little furry beast?" I ask. I grab her hips, slowing her down, making her roll against me harder and longer.

"Yup." She gives a giggle.

I slap her ass. "What have I told you about that?" I plant a trail of teasing kisses down her neck, nipping at her collarbone.

"Mmm…" She breathes out a little moan. The sexy sound turns to a strange one, more like a groan. "Unh…"

"You don't like that?" I roll my hips, building up my rhythm, trying to get her back to that place of pleasure she was a moment ago. "You like this?"

"I think…" Her fingernails sink into my shoulders, digging into my bare flesh. "I'm… I'm… I'm going to be sick."

Huh? God, it feels so good, being inside her. It makes my head feel cloudy. I must have misheard her.

"What?" I give a moan, dipping deeper inside her. "You mean you're going to come?"

She bites her lips, shaking her head as her face turns to alabaster.

Then, she throws up. Every bite she took of Chef's pasta.

All over me.

CHAPTER
TWENTY-FIVE

Charlie

Another little plus sign. A tiny purplish-pink symbol that will forever change my life. Again. I hold the white plastic test in my hand, tears filling my eyes. I don't know how a heart can be so filled with hope and sorrow at the same time, but that's what I'm experiencing.

Of course, the moment the positive result appears, that sudden burst of surprised joy launches from your chest to your throat, making your fingers flutter in front of your mouth, your words choke into silence.

But for me, the immediate second wave of thoughts and feelings plow through. What if this is another false pregnancy? Will I be strong enough to survive that horrific moment when the doctor's face goes blank and they look at me and shake their head, telling me there's no baby there?

He's standing behind me, my rock, my constant support. His hands are wrapped around my waist. He holds me, glancing down over my shoulder. "Plus. That's good news, right?"

I shake my head. "We don't know. Not yet."

He laughs, taking the stick from me to inspect it closer. "No, baby. This is positive. That's good."

"Don't you want to see if this one… takes… first." I blink back tears. "Before we marry? Before we celebrate?"

I watch him in the bathroom mirror as he bends down, kissing the top of my head. "Hell no. If there's a plus on that pregnancy test, it's my baby. For a second, for a minute, for a lifetime." He shakes his head. "It doesn't matter. It's mine."

"That's sweet." I squeeze his hand. He looks like he wants to roll his eyes, but he holds back. He's getting used to me calling him sweet.

"Look, baby, I know you can't rest—with good reason—until we get confirmation that there really is a baby growing in your belly. I'm calling Dr. Williams right now and we're going to go see her as soon as possible."

Only one of the reasons I love him so much. He knows exactly what I need, and he makes it happen. A few hours later, we're sitting in the medical room in the castle. Dr. Williams has my legs covered in warm quilts, my belly exposed for her inspection.

Dr. Williams does an external check, her doppler sliding over the warm jelly she's spread on my belly. She can see I'm holding my breath, expecting the worst.

She gives me a smile. "I'm finding the heartbeat," she says. "Give it a minute. Try to breathe."

"Finding? Or searching for?" I ask. I've been through this before, the doctor searching while I held my breath, then him finding nothing. I feel uncomfortable, prickles of heat dancing over my lower back as I lie on the bed.

Dr. Williams's brown eyes lock on mine. "I'm locating the active heartbeat of your healthy baby, sweetheart."

A loud *swish-swish-swish* comes over the doppler. The heartbeat is much faster than mine would sound. It belongs to my baby.

Doesn't it?

A huge smile, bright as the sun, spreads over Dr. Williams's face. "See? There it is. Strong as can be."

We listen for a moment, Nikolaos's hand squeezing mine. It's literally the most amazing sound in the whole world. The strong heartbeat of my real live baby. I can't believe I'm hearing my baby's heartbeat.

"See?" He kisses my cheek. "Curse is broken."

"Curse?" Dr. Williams's nose wrinkles up. "What curse?"

"Nothing." I shake my head. "Just a silly inside joke."

"Okay," Dr. Williams says, "It's time to move on to the internal ultrasound. Let's check out what's going on with this little peanut."

"Oh my gosh, I can't believe we're actually going to be able to see our baby." Nikolaos holds onto my shoulder as Dr. Williams cleans the jelly from my belly, fixing my top back in place. She helps me spread my legs under the quilt, inserting the wand of the internal ultrasound.

She says, "Some would use an external ultrasound at this point, but I know how stressed you've been, and I want to give you the clearest picture possible to ease your mind."

"I can handle whatever you throw at me."

As long as I leave here with a picture of my precious, healthy baby.

She finds the baby, a little tiny being showing up on the screen. There's a flickering heartbeat in its little rib cage. You can make out the early formations of little hands and feet, the baby curled in a curve, looking snug.

"Oh my gosh. Oh my gosh." I'm overwhelmed. There's a baby in there. A real, live baby.

The doctor uses her tools to measure the baby. "8.5 centimeters. Perfect size for fourteen weeks. About the size of a precious little kiwi fruit. Baby is kicking around but you won't be able to feel it yet."

"Fourteen weeks!"

Shock and surprise settles over me. How on earth could I have been pregnant for fourteen weeks and not realized it?

Sure, my waistband has expanded a bit, but I'd put the blame on Remy's good cooking and the fact that Nikolaos has chocolate from Lush on auto-ship. The fatigue I've been feeling? I glance over at Nikolaos who, in his newfound state of "daddy," looks even more handsome than before.

Didn't think that was possible…

But yes, his hot body and sexy demeanor have kept us very active in the bedroom, the riverboat, the greenhouse, the stairs of the castle. I'd blamed my fatigue on him.

Fourteen weeks…

"Oh no. I had a glass of wine last night. And one last week as well. Will the baby be okay?"

She nods. "One or two glasses of wine before you found out you were pregnant won't hurt baby. But I'd recommend you abstain from now on."

Nikolaos gives her a look so serious I almost laugh. "There won't be any alcohol near this baby."

"Will I be able to feel it move soon?" I ask.

"Yes." She nods. "Around sixteen to twenty-four weeks."

Nikolaos beams. "I can't wait to put my hand on your belly and feel the kick of our baby girl."

"Girl?" I shoot him a curious look. Did he see something on the screen that I missed? "How do you know it's a girl?"

He gives a big shrug. "I just know. I've known since that little pink plus sign showed up."

"You do know that all the tests are pink, right? Pink doesn't mean a girl. It just tells you you're pregnant," I say.

"I know." He gives a lopsided grin. "But just wait and see. I'm right."

"*Wellll....*" Dr. Williams gets a sly smile on her face. "I mean, it's really early to be determining these things, but Nikolaos does own the most advanced ultrasound machine on the market, sooo... if you want to know what I think you're having, I'd be happy to give you my best guess."

We came straight here after getting the positive test. We haven't had the capacity to discuss gender reveals. I glance up at Nikolaos. "Do we want to know?"

"Hell yes, we do. I need to know if I'm buying a pink or blue four-wheeler for the property."

"No four-wheelers," I laugh. "But yes. Tell us. What do you think?"

Dr. Williams stares at the screen for a moment, then beams at Nikolaos. "You're right, daddy. Best I can tell, you two are having a girl."

"Oh my gosh. A little girl." My mind instantly fills with mommy-daughter talks, daddy-daughter dances, and, of course, pink floral prints.

"Told you. See, we already have a connection." He leans down, his breath rustling my hair. "And she told me to tell you she already loves you."

"Oh my." I dab at the tears welling in my eyes. "You really are sweet, aren't you?"

"The sweetest." He kisses the top of my head.

I glance up at him, loving the look on his face as he stares at our baby on the screen. "I love you."

"Love you too, baby."

After Dr. Williams leaves, he books a boat to take us to the mainland, to go straight to the city. He takes me to Clara's Children's Boutique, the family's kids' clothing store, a brownstone on the exterior wall of the Village.

Every single item and article of clothing that I give so much as an "aww" or second glance, he buys. The staff packs everything up in pink tissue paper and white boxes to send back to the island for us. Then, he takes me to lunch at Buon Cibo, a little Italian restaurant the family likes to frequent. The chicken parmesan is everything I've been craving.

For dessert we hit Lush. We sit sipping our coffees—he triple-checked with the barista that mine was decaf before he handed it to me—and taste testing chocolates. He hates chocolate but he's more than happy to accompany me and keep half of the sweets in front of him, so I don't look like such a pig.

He's such a sweetheart.

When I've had my fill, he has the leftovers boxed up to take home, knowing how much I miss Lush. Honestly, I looove my friends, I love New York, but I really don't miss living in the city. The quiet peace of Dark Island soothes my soul. The fun of the adventure of living in a castle hasn't yet worn off and I don't think it ever will.

We sit for a moment, relaxing in the cute chocolate shop. I twist my ring around my finger, a new habit I've acquired.

He looks down at my ring. "So, how soon can we make that happen?"

My hand goes to my belly. "I don't know. Now with our amazing surprise on the way... should we marry before or after baby comes?"

"There's no question. Before." His brows go sky high, his tone dropping into the non-negotiable zone. "You will be my wife when you have my baby."

"Okay, okay." I laugh. "We'll marry before."

"If I had my way, we'd already be married," he grumbles.

"We need time to plan a wedding. There's a lot that goes into such a big event," I say.

"I'm not going to relax till I get a wedding band on your finger. I have a way to make it happen without stressing you out."

"How?" I ask.

He waggles his brows mischievously. "I have a secret weapon."

CHAPTER
TWENTY-SIX

Beast

Ashely has been my right-hand woman for the past year. She came to me from Bryant Bachman, one of the daddy doms of the family who lives at The West in Manhattan. He runs a successful tech company and Ashely was his PA. He couldn't speak more highly of her than he did when he called me to ask if I needed a Bachman-friendly employee to help me run things at the castle.

Apparently, Ashely had a bit of a crush on him and was broken-hearted when he found the woman of his dreams in a young woman named Reece. Ashely put in her notice and started looking for jobs, but Bryant didn't want the family to lose her, she's too valuable. Every day I'm grateful she's here. Her organizational skills and get-it-done attitude are the main reason the interior of the castle is exactly how I want it.

When we found out the modern style chandeliers I wanted were collection only, Ashely took a weekend trip to Italy to retrieve them. When I found my dream thirty-five-foot riverboat for the waterway boathouse, it needed work, and Ashely found a man on the mainland to take care of it, a recluse with a long gray mustache and a plaid driver's cap always perched on the top of his head. He lives in a cabin at the edge of the shore, spending his days bringing boats like mine back to life. When we needed donations of clothing and accessories for the women, Ashely went to the city to pack everything up and bring it down, never asking a single question as to why I needed those things.

I wouldn't put Charlie in the position of planning a wedding this quickly if I didn't have Ashely's help. She's that good. And one thing I will not do, no matter how much I want my ring on her finger and the word "husband" on her lips, is stress out the mother of my child.

"How on earth are we going to pull off throwing a wedding before this little one arrives?" Charlie asks. "What's your secret weapon?"

"Ashely," I say. "Ashely can work magic."

"She is amazing, isn't she?" Charlie's brow knits as she rubs her belly. "How soon are you thinking?"

"Four weeks," I say. "It's the most I can do."

"Four weeks!" Her jaw falls open. "That's unheard of. Even for someone like Ashely."

"She can handle it. Trust me. We'll talk to her, but in the meantime, let's go do the fun stuff."

"Like what?" she asks.

I want to get something done today. We need to get started on this wedding. Ashely is obsessed with weddings and working alongside her, I've received an education that could give me a PhD in event planning.

I think of the family shops. "We could get the cake chosen and ordered. And, if you wouldn't mind me seeing it ahead of time, we could go down to Daughtry's and pick out the dress."

Her nose wrinkles adorably as she gives it a think. "Hmm... well, to be honest, I don't want to do anything without you. If you saw my dress ahead of time, it wouldn't bother me. I mean, plus, I'm already pregnant. That's out of the norm too." She smiles. "I actually really love the idea of you and me shopping together. I want to know you love the dress."

"Then it's settled. Let's go." I stand, grabbing her coat from the back of her chair and helping her slip into it.

We start with the dress. Daughtry's has racks of white, ivory, and cream-colored gowns. Any one of them would look lovely on her.

The saleswoman sees us browsing the dresses and approaches us, giving me a curious look. "Groomsman?"

"Groom groom," I say.

"Oh, that's unusual. Just a moment." She rushes off, returning with two glasses of champagne.

I take both glasses, sinking down into the cushy leather chair that's calling my name. I sip on champagne and wait while Charlie and the saleswoman choose a few dresses for Charlie to try.

When she steps out in the first dress, I'm almost brought to tears. The silky white fabric shimmers as it hugs the curves of her body; her slightly rounded belly protrudes adorably. A silver sash rests just above her waist, the ties trailing elegantly behind her.

She looks like a goddess. The prettiest thing I've ever seen.

She gives me a shy smile. "You like it?"

"Damn." I set the glasses down on the table beside me and stand. "You look stunning."

I'm torn between wanting to grab her in my arms and hold her, careful in how I touch the dress for fear I'll mess it up, and wanting to tear it off her and relieve the stirring in my cock that started the moment I saw her in the dress. "I think that's the one."

She gives a little twirl, the hem of the dress swishing around her ankles. "Are you sure?"

"Yes. If you love it as much as I do, then yes."

She shines, she sparkles, her natural beauty only enhanced by the dress. "Alright." She turns to the saleswoman. "We'll take it."

They make plans for one slight alteration in the otherwise perfect dress: room for my growing baby.

The saleswoman gives a satisfied nod. "I'll have it altered, steamed, and sent to your address."

We move on to the bakery, feeding one another bites of different flavors of cakes. We both like the plainest one best. Now, it's time to talk to Ashely.

We head home. The breeze from the boat ride whips Charlie's hair around her smiling face. I keep my arm around her shoulders, wanting to block the wind and keep her warm.

Ashely's waiting for us in the library with a roaring fire and a hot coffee for me, a hot chocolate for Charlie. She sits across from us in a chair she's pulled over. Folding her hands in her lap demurely, she says, "What did you two want to talk to me about?"

"We need a miracle," I say. "And I think you're the only person who can make it happen."

"Oookay..." she says slowly. "And just what is this miracle?"

"We need our wedding planned," Charlie says.

At the word wedding, Ashely's eyes instantly glow with excitement.

"In four weeks," I add.

"Oh. Oookay." She nods, taking a minute to absorb the idea. "Okay." She gives a more definitive nod. "We can do this. We can do this. I can do this."

Her eyes lock on mine, her gaze as serious as a military leader preparing their next battle move. "What are you thinking for location? Here at the castle? The Village? The Parrish?"

We both say, "Here. The castle," at the same time.

"Jinx!" Charlie laughs. "I'm so happy we are on the same page. I couldn't imagine us getting married anywhere else."

"Me either."

"Okay, that's done." Ashely nods with relief. "And the reception, what are you thinking of for the reception? Morning? Evening? Indoor, outdoor with heaters?"

"The reception?" Charlie rubs her growing belly. "I think I'd like to be surprised."

Ashely's perfectly shaped brows knit. "You mean… like… I would pick out… everything?"

"I'm just having so much fun prepping for the baby. Planning a reception seems like a lot of work." She realizes how much she's asking for and quickly adds in, "Only if you're up for it, of course. I mean, it's asking a lot—"

"Oh, no." Ashely shakes her head, her blonde hair shining. "No. No. No."

"No?" Charlie's face drops.

"I mean, no, it wouldn't be a problem. My answer is yes!" Ashely leans forward, putting a hand over Charlie's. "It's an event planner's dream come true. Truly. What makes us so great at our job is how much we love having control over everything, so to get to be the one to pick it all out, dream it all up?" Her eyes light with excitement, plans already churning in her mind. "I'm thrilled."

"If you're sure," Charlie says. "I'd love that. If it's okay with you, of course?" Charlie looks at me.

I give a nod and a grunt.

Ashely says, "I know Nikolaos's taste very well by now. And I feel like I've gotten to know yours. I'll come to you if there're any questions I have, or if I'm on the fence about something, but other than that, you'd like it to be a surprise? You don't want me to run everything by you first?"

"No. I trust you completely." She looks at me to be sure I'm on board. "I think a surprise would be nice. Are you really okay with that?"

I guess a grunt is not enough of a response to reassure her I like the idea too. I lean down, kissing her belly, then look back up at her. "I want whatever makes you happiest."

Charlie gives me a look of love. "I'd like the surprise. Thank you so much, Ashely. I'm so happy you're excited."

"Oh, I am." Ashely nods. "I'm thrilled. This will be a night to remember, and I don't want you to worry over a single thing. You'll for sure be a bride who actually gets to enjoy her wedding day."

Toward the end of the meeting I can see that Charlie's energy is waning. This has been a huge, emotional, happy day and with the onset of early pregnancy fatigue, combined with all the shopping and planning, my baby is fading fast.

"I'll be in touch later today to help you get started," I tell Ashely, helping Charlie from her chair. "I think right now I'd better get mama upstairs for some rest."

"Of course. Be well and don't spend one moment stressing about this wedding. I'll have it all under control. You just focus on keeping the baby safe and cozy." Ashely leans over, kissing —Charlie's cheek.

We get up to our bedroom where I help her out of her clothing. The sight of her body, the small signs of her surprise pregnancy now clear to me—her fuller breasts, the curve of her belly—turns me on to no end.

Charlie Bachman, the woman that I haven't been able to get out of my mind since the first moment I set eyes on her, is carrying my child. I slide my arms around her naked body, needing to be close to her.

I rub my hand over her belly, burying my face in her hair and inhaling her scent. "How about a warm bath to relax?"

She leans back against me, melting into me. "Mmm… that sounds amazing."

I slip a thick robe around her shoulders to keep her warm while I draw the bath. I pull my shirt up over my head, catching her staring at me from the bathroom door. She loves my tattoo. Loves to watch me undress. I take off the rest of my clothing, slowly, offering her the show I know she wants.

I step into the tub, the warm water swirling around my feet. Steam rises around me as I slip down into the tub.

"Come. Join me."

Shyly, she tiptoes over, shrugging out of her robe. I'll never tire of seeing her naked body, no matter the shape or size of it. I reach my arms up, helping her to step in between my legs. I hold her hips steady and lower her down in front of me.

The tub is plenty big enough for two and the perfect size for her to nestle against me. A perfect fit. I can't help the erection that immediately rises, digging into the cleft of her ass. I promise, my fulfillment was not my intention.

I just want to relax my bride, make her feel good.

She wiggles against my cock. "Mmm… someone's feeling happy."

My cock wants her, but I want her to relax. "I want you to be happy." I pull the pivoting tap toward her until the stream of water is flowing between her thighs.

She's surprised by the thrum of the warm water flowing over her sex. "Oh!" She melts into me, her back resting against my chest.

I slip my arms around her waist, my fingers parting her sex, allowing the stream of water to massage her clit. "Let all the stress of the day go, baby. Just relax."

"Mmm…" Her hips roll against the insides of my thighs, my cock nestling against the softness of her ass.

I let the water do its work, holding her in place. She shifts and moans. "Oh my goodness…"

Her back curves away from me as her body tenses in the warm water. Her pretty face is flushed, the ends of her damp hair clinging to her skin. Her lips part, her knees twitch as the orgasm shudders through her.

Watching her come makes all my selfless ideas of only pleasuring her melt from my mind. She's so beautiful when she comes, and the feel of her ass against my cock, it's too much.

"Come here, baby." I turn her to face me, putting her on her knees so she's straddling me with her knees on the outsides of my thighs. I grab the bottle of almond oil from the wooden tray that balances across the far end of the tub. Lifting my hips, I stroke oil on my cock as she stares. I love when she watches me stroke my cock.

Her hands grip the sides of the tub. I grab her hips, guiding her on top of me. Her eyes fall closed, her head lolling back as she slowly lowers herself onto my cock.

I want her eyes on mine. I run a thumb over her chin. "Look at me."

"Mmm...kay." Her eyes flutter open, a slow, sexy smile of satisfaction spreading over her face as I fill her with my cock.

"God, you're so tight and warm and wet. You feel so fuck—" It feels weird dropping an f-bomb in front of the baby despite what I'm currently doing with her mother. I correct myself. "You feel so damn good, baby."

Using the sides of the tub as her anchor, she slowly lifts then lowers herself again, moaning as she does. I lift my hips, burying inside of her. I go gentle, I'll always be gentle till the day our baby girl is born and Charlie's fully healed.

"That feels so, so good."

"Did you have a good day, baby?"

"The best. I can't believe we're going to have a baby. And a wedding."

I stroke her breasts, cupping their soft weight in my palms. Her nipples come to life at my touch, lush buds for me to taste. I lean forward, kissing and sucking on her nipples. She runs a hand through my hair, rocking her hips forward and back.

Her pace quickens as she finds that sweet place where the orgasm begins to build. She feels so good, her breasts feel so good, she looks so damn gorgeous sitting up there on my lap, riding my cock, I have to take deep, deep breaths to hold back. I don't want to come till she does.

This whole bath was supposed to be for her, after all.

Not my fault my wife-to-be is too damn sexy for her own good.

The tightness in my balls takes my breath away. I cling to her, my body curving around hers as the freight train comes rushing into the station. I can't hold back any longer, the tension in my core building past the point of no return.

Her words come breathy and sweet. "I'm coming…"

Oh. Thank. God.

I let go.

"Grrr…" Growling into her collarbone, her wet hair clinging to my face, I experience the strongest climax of my life. Her being pregnant, her becoming my wife, her being my partner for life… and I get to share moments like *this* with her too?

My mind experiences its own peak of pleasure as the aftershocks of our orgasms tremble through us. I search for her lips, needing her kiss. Our mouths meet in a slow, lazy kiss, the warm glow from our bodies seeping into our embrace.

CHAPTER
TWENTY-SEVEN

Charlie

The boathouse, the one with the riverboat and waterway, has been transformed for our wedding ceremony. White lights hang from the ceiling's wood beams. The waterway runs between two strips of concrete. The one across from the boat is covered in paper luminarias, their cut-outs different shapes of plants, candlelight flickering from their leaves. The concrete ground has been strewn in rose petals, red, pinks, corals, and whites.

My favorite decoration?

Ashely dotted the water with big, wide, circular white floating candles and big blossoms of water lilies, their white petals so pretty against their shiny green leaves. I wish she could be here to see them in our special moment, but Ashely won't be able to be at the ceremony. We've opted for a Bachman family-only event, since neither of us have close ties with anyone outside of our chosen family, but she'll be at the reception.

I know what she's going to tell us. She's quitting. Either she's insanely professional or Nikolaos is crazy oblivious, but I've heard through the staff gossip line that the teeny tiny hint of jealousy I was detecting from her was real. Poor girl was crushing on her boss.

Can I blame her?

Certainly not. I think everyone should have a crush on my man. He's amazing. I wish she would stay on, but I understand why she wants a fresh start. No matter what she goes on to do, I'll be forever grateful to her for the beauty she's brought to our special day.

The family stands on the other concrete strip, and Nikolaos, Rockland, and I are on the little deck of the riverboat as it floats in the water.

The dress still fits perfectly, just a tad snug around my baby belly. I've chosen to wear my hair back in a low, loose romantic knot, a huge white orchid tucked to the right of the knot. I brought my pearls from home, and they hang around my neck, giving me comfort like an old friend. He wears a simple navy suit with a cream-colored shirt beneath. He, my giant mafia beast, has donned the pink tie Ashely insisted he wear to match our colors.

Real men wear pink, he said to me, taking the tie from Ashely and giving me a kiss.

He'd do anything to make this day perfect for me.

Nikolaos gifted me with three-carat each diamond studs this morning and they sparkle in my earlobes. I've chosen not to have a wedding party, or something old, something new, something borrowed, something blue.

Simple. Keep it simple and have a good time. And no talk of curses. That's what Nikolaos has been saying since the day we began planning and I've stuck to it.

Cursed? How can I be cursed? I stare at his handsome face, the warm light of the water shining over him, making him truly look like the Greek god status that he's reached in my life.

We hold hands and the whole world melts away as Rockland starts to speak. It feels like we're the only two people in the world, and that this is a private moment between us. I've heard Rockland speak these familiar words before, but today they feel different. The last time I stood at this altar, I stood with a good man who I knew wanted to take care of me.

Today, I stand with my soulmate.

The words are so beautiful, and I feel them so deeply, they bring tears to my eyes.

"These words spoken today are sacred and celebrate a lasting bond that already exists between Charlie and Nikolaos, who have already joined their hearts together and chosen to walk together on life's journey. Today, as Bachmans, we bear witness to the pledge of a sacred, eternal bond. One that may not be broken. Nikolaos, please declare your vows."

He holds both my hands in his, his eyes never moving from mine as he recites his vows to me. "I, Nikolaos, take you, Charlie, to be my wife; to have and to hold, from this day forward; for better, for worse; for richer, for poorer; in sickness and in health; to love and to cherish; until we are parted by death."

I can't stop the smile that's beaming from my face. I feel giddy, almost silly with excitement. I can't wait to say the words, to make him mine. Joy flows through my voice as I repeat the same promises back to him. "I, Charlie, take you, Nikolaos, to be my husband; to have and to hold from this day forward. I vow to accept your leadership over our family. To obey your word. To accept your discipline. For better, for worse; for richer, for poorer; in sickness and in health; to love and to cherish; until we are parted by..." My throat closes, thinking of that damned curse I'd promised to leave behind, but I swallow back my fear and finish. "Death."

Nikolaos gives me a kiss and leaves me on the deck of the boat with Rockland. He steps up onto the concrete, going to one of the brothers to get the box and the candle.

This is the part that most brides would be nervous about, their first time experiencing the family ceremony, their belly in knots, not knowing what to expect. For me, I've been to dozens of these ceremonies, so it's nothing but pleasant.

I've always loved the way we cut the lights. The luminarias and floating candles still offer a soft glow but the white lights overhead as well as the ones down in the waterway go out.

We stand in the dark, in a reverent silence for a few moments while candles are passed around. Nikolaos walks back over, carrying a tall, flickering white pillar candle in one hand, a small red leather jewelry box in the other.

He lights Rockland's candle and from there, the flame spreads, dozens of candles fill the boathouse with light, their flickering flames reflecting off the water. When all of the candles are lit, Nikolaos hands his to Rockland so he can open the little box.

I've been so calm, so peaceful this whole time, but when he goes to open the little red leather jewelry box with those scrolling gold letters spelling Bachman across the top, I'm terrified. My heart pounds, my breaths come too fast. The memory of my husband's death, the fear of losing him...

It all comes rushing over me at once. I feel lightheaded, swaying on my high heels.

"All Bachman women wear this necklace. It is a symbol of our creed, the way we live our lives, the eternal care of a man for a woman. For as long as the stars have lit the sky, men have cared for and loved the women they have pledged their lives to. And women have loved and obeyed those men, accepting them as the headship of their family. Choosing to give the gift of their submission to these men—men who would lay down their lives for the ones they love. The sword is our symbol — the length we are willing to go to, the sacrifice we would willingly make.

"Charlie, I freely give you this symbol, and pledge my very life to you. Do you accept?"

"Yes, of course." My fingers go to the little charm. It hangs just below the flower pendant I've still not taken off.

"Fire," Rockland says, "also as timeless as the Earth, symbolizes the Bachman family's pledge to one another. To guide, care for, and protect one another above all others. Bachmans, do you accept the union of Charlie and Nikolaos?"

"We do."

"And Bachmans, do you pledge to care for and protect this bride and groom, as you would your own blood?"

"We do."

"And how long will you hold these two in your care?"

"Forever."

I dab the tears from my eyes as Nikolaos hugs me tight, kissing the top of my head. Hand in hand, we leave the room to make our way to the castle. Our reception will be the first to be held in the castle's ballroom. I can't wait to see what Ashely's come up with. The family follows us into the cool air of the night, light laughter and chatting swirling around us as we navigate the path.

Single brothers dressed in black tuxes stand on either side of the big, wide doors.

Ashely's there too. She offers me a quick hug, then steps back. She gestures to the doors like a game show attendant. "Welcome to your happily ever after, Charlie."

The young men swing the doors open in unison, revealing our celebration.

I knew Ashely would make it beautiful, but this is breathtaking. I give a little gasp. "Oh my gosh! It's incredible."

Nikolaos squeezes my hand, guiding me around the room to take it all in. His touch grounds me, makes my earlier lightheadedness dissipate.

The room has been transformed into a garden. Fat globe lights fan out, strung from the center of the ceiling. Beneath them hangs clear netting holding hundreds of white roses and pale pink Peruvian lilies, giving the effect of flowers floating above our heads.

There's a stage set up at the front of the room. Tall, blooming rose bushes cover the stage, standing proudly in their huge wooden planters. A band waits at the corner of the stage, their matching green tuxes and gowns dotted with pink bow ties and sashes or cummerbunds.

I'm looking forward to that first dance, ready to relive the feeling of our first dance together at Kylie's wedding. The band will play our song, "Falling Like the Stars." We chose it because it reminds us of nights spent on the veranda of the castle, the sky a blanket of a thousand stars above our heads.

My chocolate and flower wall inventions are here, chocolates floating amongst big bright pink begonias and lush greenery. The cake we chose from the bakery sits on a dessert table in front of the chocolate walls, a three-tiered classic white cake with white frosting. The cake topper is a sweet surprise, a tiny little man and woman, the woman holding one hand to her adorable baby bump. There're mini cupcakes, pink and green sprinkles dotting their white frosting, as well as white trays of pink and green macarons.

My one request was, with this being my second wedding, I wanted it a bit more casual. No announcements, no speeches, no sit-down dinner.

Flowering trees were brought in, forming a wall behind the long tables of food. Remy did all the food. An army of helpers worked under his direction for the past week. Each dish is plated on small white plates, dotting the tabletops, ready for people to grab. Scallops, lobster, duck foie gras, green salads, thin slices of smoked salmon, and delicate cuts of beef tenderloin.

The classic Beauty champagne tower stands in the corner by the bar. Casual seating is offered, high top tables with two to four seats, each of their tops adorned with a glass vase holding a white and pink bouquet, a green satin ribbon tied around each vase.

Ashely appears at my side, handing me a sparkling water. "For the bride."

"Ashely, this is so beautiful. I love it so much. I can't thank you enough." I pull her in for another quick hug. "I can't wait to help you with yours, one day."

"You know what they say." She gives a choked laugh. "Always the wedding planner, never the bride."

She's so sweet, so caring. "You'll find your person one day, I just know it." I nod toward the group of younger single brothers gathering around the bar, glasses of whiskey in their hands. "Might even be a Bachman man."

"Wouldn't that just be the dream?" She gives me a sweet smile. "Enjoy your night. Let me know if you need anything at all."

The first few notes of our song fill the room.

Nikolaos holds his hand out to me. "May I have this dance?"

I giggle at his formality. "You may." I slip my hand in his.

He leads me to the dance floor. The band plays our song. And we dance.

For the first time, as husband and wife, our baby tucked safely between us.

And I'm head over heels in love with both of them.

My little family.

EPILOGUE

Charlie

I'm sipping tea in the garden, the sun warming my skin. I glance down at my ring, remembering the speech Nikolaos made on the shore when he proposed five years ago.

Two little girls, four and three years of age, their blonde curls bouncing, run through the flower-lined paths, squealing. They're being chased by the big, bad beast and if he captures them, he'll tickle them till they beg for mercy.

My hand goes to my belly. Today, over tea cakes and tiny sandwiches, we'll be telling the girls that they're finally going to outnumber us. They've been begging for a sibling, especially our eldest, and today they'll find out their wish is coming true.

I take good care of those little girls. The best I can. I know I'm a good mother. I've gained confidence in myself since having them, working hard to provide for them, giving them everything I didn't have in my own childhood. Those little girls will never want for love, attention, or care.

The Beast makes a quick stop in his quest, planting a kiss on my lips. He whispers in my ear, "You look beautiful, Mama," and gives my belly a little rub. He rumbles up a deep growl, resuming the chase.

It's going to be a little boy. My baby beast. He'll be his own little person, but I'd be lying if I said I wasn't hoping he'll look just like his father.

The curse is broken.

I've reached my happily ever after.

And now I'll never, ever be alone.

Second Epilogue

Ashely

I'm a hard worker. A smart woman. A decent dresser.

I have one teensy tiny bad habit. Okay, it's beyond bad.

It's deplorable.

I tend to fall in love with my bosses. And vice versa.

It's happened not once, but twice. I work with them every day, help them with all their problems, serve them, and through the process, they fall absolutely head over heels for me.

Then they find their one true love. And I'm forced to move on.

My latest boss, Nikolaos, has found his love in Charlie. And I truly couldn't be happier for them both. Charlie is sweet and kind and achingly beautiful and she deserves every happiness.

Which is why I need to move on.

I hate the idea of leaving Dark Island, but just like in my first job, I need to. I've packed my bags, and I'm headed to a place I've only heard stories about.

The Village in New York.

I'm not a Bachman, I'm not even dating one, but the family trusts me enough to hire me as Tess's personal assistant. She heard I'm the best and she only hires the best.

And for the first time in my life, I'm truly relieved my boss is a woman.

There's absolutely no chance of me falling in love with my boss this time.

None at all.

But then, in walks Boston "Boss" Bachman.

New England royalty. Billionaire stud. Mafia man.

Dangerous. Punishing. Dark.

My total opposite. And guess what?

Tess has handed me off. Making him my new boss.

Is she playing matchmaker?

Third time must be the freaking charm because I'm pretty sure:

Unlike my first two bosses, this man is obsessed with me.

Hello, lovely Reader!

Ashely will be getting her own book, soon. Sign up for my newsletter to be informed of it's release:

www.shannahandelromance.com

About the Author

SHANNA HANDEL
Romance

Shanna Handel is an internationally bestselling author of over 50 romance novels. She is currently living her own, hard-won happily ever after.

Sign up for Shanna's newsletter to hear about new releases:

https://www.shannahandelromance.com/

Follow Shanna on Amazon:

https://author.to/ShannaHandelRomance

You can keep up with Shanna Handel via her Facebook group, her Facebook page, and her Goodreads profile:

Shanna's Reader Group

Shanna Handel Romance Page

Follow Shanna on Goodreads

Follow Shanna on Bookbub